So much positive stuff happens in this city every day that its unreal. Black people and white people are not strangling each other on sight, drug crazed gang members are not blazing away with Uzi's on every corner, the African-Americans here are not being left out of the political process and we are not going to hell this afternoon.

Sometimes I feel like screaming when I feel that I'm being saturated with all of the negative stuff. It comes from many directions; the media mostly, and from people who buy into the negative and spread it around.

No, of course, this is not paradise. We do have problems. That's intrinsic to city life.

But I refuse to allow the negative blinders to blot the positive picture art. We help each other here, people are ready, willing and able to do what they can to help the other person.

That's not an unusual thing, people do it ordinarily. We share. I think the greatest testimonial to the facts that most people in this city have their heads screwed on right is the fact that the city works.

If we were as messed up as some folks want to make us believe, we'd be up to our necks in shit. I rest my case.

BLACK CHICAGO

ODIE HAWKINS

Originally published by Holloway House Publishing Co.

Copyright © 1992, 2011 by Odie Hawkins

Front cover photo by Zola Salena-Hawkins,
www.flickr.com/photos/32886903@N02

ISBN: 978-1-5040-3580-4

Distributed in 2016 by Open Road Distribution
180 Maiden Lane
New York, NY 10038
www.openroadmedia.com

Dedications

To brother Jean Baptiste Point Du Sable, for creating it.
To Dr. Margaret Burroughs, for being herself.
To the memory of Mayor Harold Washington.
To Martha, David and Heather, for being
warm and sensitive.
To Fred and Lynn, who gave me the garden
when the streets got hot.
To the brothers and sisters of Chicago,
especially David Hawkins.
and
To Bo' Felt; a friend, comrade of the night runs and A
MAN who has shared Aphrodisiacal atmospheres,
loaned me money, offered superior advice and proven,
over the years, that you don't have to have the
same blood to be a brother...
Thanks to Elenore Slaughter-Williams for being a
dynamite copy cat.
(A special hug to Ralph Carrington for carrying me back
and forth.) The mistakes are all mine. And finally, to
Adalisha Safi, for her good vibes and sensitivity.

BLACK
CHICAGO

Prologue

Jean Baptiste Point Du Sable, a fur trapper and a sharp cookie in the business world, was the founder of Chicago.

He was born in St. Marc, Saint Domingue (it was renamed Haiti in 1804), the son of a Frenchman and a African born woman who had been enslaved. There are a number of different stories told about his life but the first authentic information comes from Colonel Arrent de Peyster, a British officer who was in command of the region which included what is now Chicago.

De Peyster wrote; "a handsome Negro, Baptiste Point Du Sable, well educated and settled at Eschikagou, but was much in the interest of the French."

Colonel de Peyster suspected that Du Sable was playing hanky-panky with England's enemies and "detained" him under suspicion of "treasonable intercourse with the enemy."

Somehow Du Sable escaped and was arrested again. A charming devil, he made such an impression on the British governor, Patrick Sinclair, that he had him released and placed in charge of a settlement on the St. Clair River, south of Port Huran, where he remained until 1784.

The profile of a very clever brother begins to emerge. How do you go from being guilty of "treasonable intercourse with the enemy" to working for the people who have accused you?

During this same time frame he acquired 800 acres of land

in Peoria. He returned to his ol' stomping ground (Eschikagou) in 1784, and lived there for sixteen years, where he sold his property for $1,200.00, a lot of bread for that time.

He never returned to Chicago and probably lived from 1805 to 1814 around St. Charles, Missouri, according to real estate records. (June, 1813, he transferred a house, lot and other property to his granddaughter, Eulalie Derais.)

Sadly, he was almost penniless when he died in St. Charles (1818) and was buried in St. Charles' Borromeo Cemetery.

Let's take a deeper look. There's every possibility that Du Sable, like other free people of color, may have been educated in Paris, which would definitely have given him an edge on the white barbarians who were taking America from the Native Americans.

Truth or fiction? After a shipwreck he made his way to New Orleans and was given the protection of the French Jesuits as he made his way up the Mississippi to Chicago.

Why were they obligated to protect him? What was his relationship to that order?

In any event, substantial evidence exists of the prosperous business he did at his trading post in Eschikagou. In 1790, for example, he sold forty-one pounds of flour, twenty-nine pounds of pork, a supply of baked bread in exchange for thirteen yards of cotton cloth.

His post included a log house (forty feet by twenty-two), a lake house, a dairy, a smokehouse, poultry house, workshop, stable, barn, horse mill, and perhaps a few other buildings.

He was a multi-talented man. A linguist, he spoke French, Spanish and several American Indian languages, and was not only a trader but (by 1800) a cooper, a farmer and a miller.

In 1788, he married Catherine, a Potawatomi Indian (we can't say that she was a princess or not). They had, of course,

10

lived together prior to the marriage and had a daughter named Suzanne.

Suzanne was married (1790) to Jean Baptiste Pettetier, a son Jean Baptiste Jr., the son of Jean Baptiste pere and Catherine, settled in St. Charles, Missouri (Seems that Jean Baptiste/John the Baptist, was a popular name back in those days.)

Eulalie, later Mrs. Michael Derais, was born October 8, 1796. Catherine died sometime after 1800. There in no record of Jean Baptiste Point Du Sable remarrying.

Little puzzles: after he married Catherine there is evidence of him selling twenty-one to twenty-three specimens of European art. A trader and a trapper collecting European art? Hmmmmmmmmmmmmmm . . . .

Later he stood for election as a chief of the Indian tribes around Mackinac (the true story of how much credit is due the Native American for teaching the immigrants democracy has not been told) and lost. His defeat may have been a factor in his decision to sell out and move to St. Charles, Missouri.

Jean Baptiste Point Du Sable was obviously a very complex man, a mover and a shaker (the Indians in the area stated, "the first white man we knew was Black") and his contributions to the state of Illinois and Chicago have been understated.

In 1912 a plaque was placed at the corner of Pine and Kinzie Street in Chicago, indicating it had been the site of the first house erected in Chicago, by Du Sable.

The usual racists want to try to claim a first with their boy Kinzie, but history denies them that lie.

Another plaque (northeast approach to the Michigan Ave. bridge) across the Chicago River indicates where his trading post once stood.

This writer, an alumnus of Du Sable High School, Eschikagou, Illinois, can validate Du Sable's presence by

11

a painting entitled "The Black," which used to hang in the first floor corridor. Additionally, he was one of eight Illinoisans selected for the frieze of the Illinois Centennial Building in 1965.

The specifics have not been fully explored here, or elsewhere and they should be. Jean Baptiste Point Du Sable deserves the worldwide recognition that other men of vision and talent have received.

However, we can be certain that this will not occur as long as institutional racism is allowed to wipe out the facts.

Case in point...the catalog card for Shirley Graham's: Jean Baptiste Point Du Sable, Founder of Chicago, carries the notation "fiction."

Gimme a break.

Black Chicago
Odie Hawkins 7/91

The African sectors of Chicago have peculiar histories, consequently they have peculiar ways of dealing with things.

The Westside is a lot like southern Senegal, where people have traditionally honored the deeper reasons for persons living or dying. The Southside (maybe because it's farther away from the train station) has always had the rep' for a certain kind of cool.

Like, you went on the Westside for the Blues and came to the Southside for Jazz. It's still pretty much that way, on the Blues-Jazz circuit, but rap has done an amalgamation because it's everywhere.

In Chicago people get deeper into themselves than anywhere on the planet. Or so some people think. It may have something to do with the fact that Black people eat more catfish in Chicago than anywhere else.

There are alleys in this city that hold thousands of years of history, and have only been in existence for forty or fifty years. That's not a contradiction, no matter how it sounds.

The alley that runs parallel (east to west) to Roosevelt Road is a good example; there was a time (recently) when tons of garbage stank up the alley in the summer, giving sustenance to generations of rats, and giving adventurous garbageologists more than their share of goodies.

The alley contained more dirt than the secret activities of

13

the Truman, Eisenhower, Nixon, Kennedy, Johnson, Reagan, and Bush eras combined. This alley had more shit in it than Kissinger had secrets. And it's still there! Where is Kissinger?

During the Daley Era (the first one), Chicago was an African-American torture chamber, a southern apartheid system transplanted North. The thing about it was that so many people had been chased or fled from conditions in Mississippi, Alabama and Georgia that were so much worse, they thought they had made it to a better place.

And then it snowed on their asses, and kept on snowing. And its still doing it. It's gonna do it this winter. Bet on it.

Fortunately, with the persistence and courage that African people are well known for all over the planet, the apartheid system was dismantled and replaced by the plantation system.

The plantation system allows the Africans in Chicago to leave their Bantustans every morning, but there is a subtle agreement going on; they must return to the Bantustan every evening. They must return or run the risk of incarceration.

Los Angeles, California, was the lead dog for this setup. Problem is, that California, being larger and more segregated (money does it), could pull it off easier. The Africans in Chicago are different, (geography does it).

The tightness of the city means that its impossible to keep the Lithuanians out of the Estonian sector, or the Poles out of the Mexican section (where the Czechs used to live) or the Africans out of Beverly, which used to be basically Irish.

The African sectors of Chicago have peculiar histories and there's no telling what that history is going to be 'til we get there.

Dr. Antonio Davis

It was May 6, 1991 and I had just completed a three-day mediational Fetzer Johannesburg Riesling wine sipping Amtrak trip from sunny Los Angeles to a briskly cool evening in Chicago.

I was in town for the sole purpose of feeding on Chicago, writing a Chicago themed piece that I've lusted for, for a long time.

I was going to be staying in the Michigan Avenue mansion of Charles and Dr. Margaret Burroughs for the spring and summer.

I had arrived and staying in their home getting acquainted with Dr. Burroughs' straight to the heart of the matter attitude and Charles Burroughs' silent fight with throat cancer.

Dr. Margaret Burroughs, my ex-high school teacher and the sister who gave me the early paper to scribble on, an artistic and political legend in a city of artistic and political legends starting with: Jean Baptiste Point Du Sable, Jesse Jackson, Gwendolyn Brooks, Marva Collins, Father Clements, Harold Washington...

3806 S. Michigan Ave
Chicago, Il. 60653

Before it became the Du Sable Museum of African-American History, it was the home of Charles and Margaret Burroughs, and the assortment of talented people who share the space with them.

The official segment of the museum was moved to more spacious quarters years ago (a multi-million dollar complex on the edge of Washington Park at Fifty-Sixth and Cottage Grove Avenue), the adventurers who took our story into their own hands still live there.

Big old mansion, offering reflections of another, grander slice of time. Entering, the unmistakable odor of cat piss floods the senses for a moment, the ammonia clears the sinuses.

Morning. The Queen moves first, her focused footsteps which sound like Flamenco patterns on the hardwood floors. She is preparing for another busy day.

Conversations; muted, animated, phoned, skip thru the spacious rooms, talk of art. Important talk. Creative talk. Inspirational talk. This is an ''in'' place in the ''inner city.''

The Queen sets the pace for the house. She is mercurial, generous, fascinating, warm, cool, patient, spacey, impatient, ethical, sincere, imperialistic, dynamic, very artistic, a leader, quite, civic minded, a poet, an entrepreneur, a traveler, an African-American educator, the mentor of thousands.

The Queen, like many masters, seems to occupy an elevated plane. She is a Special Person. Unconsciously she talks down to her subjects, or at them. Or she pontificates. And it is absorbed by the conscious and the sensitive, they understand.

The Queen probably hasn't had an authentic dialogue in years because the person she used to talk with has lost his voice.

The King is slowly dying with immense dignity and sandunga. His rich grained, cigarette and wine stained voice is gone but his Presence echoes thru the halls.

They might appear to be an unlikely couple to some people, but obviously they have used the years between them wisely, to sort out how they were going to be with each other.

He has always given the impression of being the Consort, Not in any whimpish-stroll-behind-the-Queen sort of way, but as a real Consort.

They are both quite individualistic and its difficult for the outsider to understand how they've been able to pull it off, so well, so long.

More morning. The artists who live upstairs and downstairs congregate in the Olympic-sized kitchen, to sip juice, coffee, or simply to seek inspiration from the smiles and frowns on each others' faces.

They are famous, some of them, near-famous, infamous, proud and driven men. Only men?

Perhaps the Queen will not tolerate a potential rival.

She is gone suddenly, returns later, absently feeds herself and one of the lovely cats from the same plate, impulsively begins to sort thru a box of what turns out to be letters, notes, scraps of paper, requests for help, pleas for understanding, attempts to do something for a reason.

A radar scan pulls her close to the real, keeps her safe

for a moment. The moments expand, drift past, tie themselves into knots, unravel, create sections of life that could never be duplicated anywhere else.

The house is quiet at noon, only the rushing motors of cars and buses passing disturb us.

On each floor, a silent artist mulls his next painting, his next word, his next attitude, and the energy of a hot evening hasn't happened yet.

An African energy, an African-American energy-halo circles the building, grabbing even the most cynical up into the premise of dedication to raising the consciousness of the African people in America, and all others who might be sensitive to the idea of behaving in a civilized way. 3806 S. Michigan Avenue.

Thunderstorms

Juicy saliva in the jaws of heaven, warm gobs of raining crackle down, we sit near the windows pretending that we are not afraid.

One evening, after the drinking had been done, the folktales spooked out again, we sat, mesmerized by the atmospheric changes that smelled like the kind of rain that happens in Chicago.

The humidity gave way to a kind of pregnant sweat. Conversations melted, none of us felt the urge to lie any more. The truth of how great the forces beyond us were revealed in a distant flash of zigzagged spear throwing.

The unwritten fiction, unlike this narrative, is that we would silently pretend not to pray, be bold, keep our hearts from facing as the first clap of thunder ground us to quivering dust.

It came from four directions...

Paxton

It was May 6, 1991; the President had conjured up a unique way to get a little more sympathy from a submissive white nation that had just finished off a Middle Eastern surgery ("Desert Storm"), an operation promoted, paid for and won by the oil interests in the USA.

The so called "war" had been a piece 'o cake. The United States Marines and their allies (the British, the French, the Egyptians, the Dutch, the Syrians, the Saudis, and whomever else they had been able to round up (the Israelis were asked to stay out of it) had simply bombed the shit out of Baghdad and walked into Kuwait on the heels of the Iraqi retreators and took the oil wells back (burning to be sure).

No one, evidently, had counted on a Kurdish situation developing. Or that Saddam Hussein would still be the ruler of Iraq after he had gotten his ass kicked by American technology.

Bush's heart was discovered to be beating out of tempo. Who knows? It might have been the truth, but to the politically hip it seemed terribly opportune.

Just as the breath of scandle about a couple of his top guys was ("frivolous plane riding") beginning to wedge between headlines that no longer battle cried ("free Kuwait"), the President's ticker began to race itself.

It clearly gave all of the country's newspaper readers a change to experience the thrill of knowing that Dan Quayle was, indeed only a heartbeat from the Oval Office.

May 6, 1991, in Chicago and a late playing baseball had held up the evening news, the last Daley was being inaugurated and no one in the Burroughs Mansion was overjoyed.

In any event, none of it mattered to Dr. Antonio Davis, the eleven-year-old man who rang Dr. Burroughs' bell to ask if he could do some yard work, earn a couple 'o bucks for candy and hot dogs, food.

He shuffled in, thru the long corridor, from the front door to the kitchen, his dark skin ashy from the evening breezes, a clear trickle of snot easing out of his left nostril.

Dr. Antonio Davis' ("what do you want to be when you grow up?"), unhesitating he answered, "a doctor," as he fumbled with the spelling of State Street. Mother, father, and oldest sister weren't at home, his friend had gone home (if anybody wanted to stretch "home" to include the Robert Taylor Projects) and he was out in the streets, trying to help himself survive.

Whether through good fortune or prior info about the lady at 3806, he had stumbled into a place where he could receive a lot of attention, inspiration ("you want some fish?"), well designed psychological counseling and work to do.

"Come tomorrow and rake the back yard and I'll pay you. You have to do a good job now, okay?"

The agreement made, he was ushered back out with a kiss, a little endearment ("you've got pretty eyes, whose eyes do you take after? " "My father's"), a couple salami sandwiches, a piece of pie, an autographed book of poems and a stern reminder that he had a job to do after school the next day.

"You don't have to ask anybody anything, there's a rake on the side of the house."

My cute little outline for the first story of the spring series

21

fell neatly into place, it was supposed to open up on spring, the month of May, as a time of love.

"Dr." Antonio Davis never made another house call.

The bleaching season turns many eggplant colored people grayish, edges walnut skins into yellowed butter, moves brick-brown to a softened orange, creates a palette that was never supposed to happen to the faces moving quickly through the city's streets. But thats not something they've stopped to think about.

The way people step is what you notice first when you get off the train, no Hollywood shufflin', no contemplative foot dragging, none of the casual movement that we've become accustomed to in "EL-A" when we happen to be where people walk.

No, none of that happens. There is a spring to the step in Chi, a slight lean into the tape. It could quite possibly be a muscular residual from the winter snow slogging and the wind chill factor fighting.

The movement you notice and the color of the people. The colors of the moving people remain imprinted long after the people have stopped moving.

In Chicago, as in Brazil, the color spectrum wanders from soot black to cloudy white, with varied denominations in between. The only distinction that happens here that doesn't happen there is months and months of snow, ice, sleet, late buses and a climate that forces the strongest to weep on bitterly cold days.

Picture Rio De Janiero, Brazil and Chicago in January and the contrast will immediately spell out the difference.

People who need the right kind of sun can usually find enough of it in May, but barely. The severely bleached and leeched struggle thru something that mimics Count Dracula anemia. The more heavily colored offer a palette that is almost African-Impressionistic.

Even the most Eurocentric of the Eurocentrists are forced to acknowledge that the mulatto beige of their coloristic dreams could never come close to the beige that they see on Wabash Avenue and Martin Luther King Drive 'round about high noon on May 7th or thereabouts.

Real dark people, the "un-reconstituted," the chocolate-cocoa hued branch suffer the reflections of past lives, charcoal lined down through their tear lines (those rivulet areas that trickle alongside the nose, past the cheeks) and around their mouths, its as though their real selves have held onto trace lines during the bleaching season.

I didn't quite know what to think when the neighbor of my friend asked, "you went to Du Sable, didn't you?"

"Yeah, why?"

"I clipped this article about one of your high school heroes out of the paper a few weeks ago, thought I'd save it for you."

I don't know what it was about the way he said it, maybe it had something to do with a white boy assuming that he knew who my high school heroes had been.

I thanked him for the clipping, it was from a New York paper, strangely, dated 2/9/91, and the sportswriter, one of those racist liberals who would be shocked to be called that, was offering his warped version of Paxton's history.

"Several weeks ago in Chicago, a postal worker named Paxton Lumpkin died, at age 54. The name, with its crunchy alliterative juxtaposition of vowels and consonants, often brought a smile to a listener, just as Paxton Lumpkin, when he was a basketball player—so clever, so deft, so joyous, dribbling low the way Groucho Marx walked but dribbling the ball as if it were a yo-yo in his hands—brought a smile to the spectator."

It was all wrong. I wanted to shred the piece, and scream — "No! That ain't the way we saw him."

The crunchy, alliterative juxtaposition of vowels and consonants didn't bring smiles to our faces when we streamed up and down the high school corridors with him, walking meditationally slow, his somewhat battered profile tilted toward the rim of the basket.

His name was what it was, the same as Bidbody Dohicky's and Jezub Kickover's names were their names; nobody crunched or juxtaposed alliterative vowels and smiled. What makes these people say stuff like that?

But yes, he was a heroic figure to many Du Sable high school students, and to others he was a dumb jock who didn't have enough sense to go to his classes.

The hero worshippers might not have been let down when he flunked out of Indiana U. after the first semester of his sophomore year, but the normal, run of the mill achievers certainly felt that he should've been a better representative of the Du Sable student body.

The writer, Ira somebody, goes on to talk about how high school basketball teams represent "a kind of hope their stars holding out the possibilities of a glorious future.

And how the Du Sable High School Panthers were an inspiration to the Black community "demonstrating for everyone that given an opportunity any underdog, by skill and drive and wit, could come out from under."

Bullshit.

That's the kind of clownish logic that's responsible for the plight of many hundreds (perhaps thousands) of tall, young men, formerly mesomorphic (now running to wino fat) and physical types in between, milling around on ghetto street corners, usually adjacent to liquor stores, who fell for the hype that led them to believe that sports would do the trick.

The piece ends on a note of pure invention; "you knew someone from Chicago was saying recently, whenever Lump entered a room, he lit it up, like he did the basketball court.

24

He was still Paxton Lumpkin, the high school basketball star. He always will be.''

It isn't necessary to invent what Paxton Lumpkin once said, in a room that I was in, not recently; ''you know somethin, man, doin' that whole time I was yo-yoin that ball up'n down the court, I shoulda been yo-yoin my ass to classes more often. Yeahhh, that's what I should've been doin'.''

The Trees

Chicago drives a hard bargain with its trees. There are people in the city that you wouldn't want to be caught dead with. Or alive. But you feel a need to have the trees around you at all times.

Lite years ago, when we were growing up in the city, winter whipped trees, (bark skins glistening within iced glazes, icicles forming holes in the upper branches) frequently scared the shit out of us on brutally cold nights.

The trees whistled, groaned death rattles crackled like witchy old crones crackling, shadow-clawed us home from iced up romantic assignments.

Eventually, inevitably, the ice melted, the tainted snow revealed black earth, fledgling grass underneath and tree buds shyly made promising appearances.

A few weeks later the buds had become bold seducers, breezy green flirts that swayed overhead and offered freckled peeks at the sky. Flitting green leaves rustled against each other, or produced a shivering music with each humid gust of wind.

The moisture in the air dried out after a short, passionate summer. And with the loss of humidity came a dancing— dizzy palette of reds, greenish yellows, velvety browns, frosted blues, autumn.

Chicago drives a hard bargain with its trees.

(Another Kind of Moulin Rouge)
Reese's the President's Lounge,
Chazz.
May 19, 1991

Men with well fashioned paunches, women with comfortable haunches, a transgenerational mix, everybody well dressed and smelling beautifully ("its called Monsieur Houbigant") fancy African—Americans ("no gym shoes allowed"), a different kind of jet set ("you going on this cruise, man?").

Its Friday night on the Southside, the spring of 1991, late. It doesn't begin to kick off til elevenish, and later.

Reese's (The Other Place, A Piece of The Rock, The Apartment, Lolisa's, The Matador Room, The Dating Game, The Continental, Swingers, Artist's, 82nd and East End, 50 Yard Line, Frances', Felix, The Enterprise, The Line Room, Boss Martin, The Safari Room, The Tiger Lounge, Palm Garden, Selzer's, The C and C Lounge, Shelter's Lounge, 87th Avalon, Percy's Palace, West Side Pick 'n Save, Westside Madison Ave, 4500 West, The Reggae Club, and a few hundred more) is the spot for a collection of "in" people.

Why? Who knows? The situations fluctuate, the circumstances change, but the people remain the same, and the people are fickle. For desperately short periods one place

27

(some would say "joint") or another will become "popular," fade in an invisible stretch and surrender to another place. There are no winners, losers, or players in this, no one becomes the head or the tail. It all just happens.

It's a bit like the dances; once it was the Walk, the Bop, the Funky Chicken, the Swim, the Monkey, the Mambo, the Twist, the Watusi, the Electric Slide.

The Electric Slide, on an officially labeled "dance floor" in the Other Place, or in an unofficially labeled dance space in Reeses...

The Tribality of it leaks thru. Here we are in 1991 and Africans in America are assembling, once again, to do something that no one else in the country has thought about doing.

In Oakland, California a Mecca of Africanity in America, it's gotten so good that top flight singers ("Who? That Li'l Short woman?") call out the steps, like a square dance caller.

The Electric Slide, as an example of what constitutes a construct of African-American aesthetics, makes for a superior example of what the deal is.

The Electric Slide is a New African Dance, (yes of course, the Old Africans do it too, but with a different vibe behind it)...women predominant, men fill in the ranks and files, the movements are seemingly loose in the sense that most African dancing seems to be "loose," but the animated and the loose bootied soon discover that they are not going to have an easy time of it if they delay the relaxation of a joint too long, or fail to catch the off rhythm, of an off rhythm. (If you miss you're gone—)

Everything is flung into the Electric Slide: fashion, it hardly makes any sense to make an attempt to get up and try to do the Electric Slide unless you're prepared to do the Electric Slide. And be dressed right.

Really simple dance, really; a motion with the left and right legs to the left front, a backward step to the side, three motions with the left shoulder, the right shoulder, a shuffle with the hips, a parking-the-can-motion with the whole body, several undefined dips and stops, a little inner play with the hands, eyes, and knee caps, all on rank and file display...

An African American Academic, a "Big Wig" (check that out, Langston Hughes), cruising thru (yeah, they do quite a bit of that in Chicago, owed the whole business into African aesthetics—we're not talking about the Motherland here, we're dealing with Africanistic aesthetics, stuff that's got to do with where we are here.

Its always stuck in my craw, the way the Caucasoid academics have always given us Brazil and Cu-ba as incredible examples of African-Afrikan retention and clearly neglected to make any attempt at an understanding of what constitutes "retention." If the Electric Slide don't do it, then li'l duck!

A certain, hip way of behaving accompanies all of this. The "clientele" drinks quite a bit, smokes ("I should've been dead quite a while back") and colors its attitudes with this New African aesthetic (transplanted, re-worked).

It colors the attitudes to the extent of weeding out the unhip (not "hep," they were never "In.") and the square.

We must go to the "Game of the Mirrors" for a real understanding of how this is understood.

Most of the places mentioned here; Reeses', The President's Lounge (#2), offer a mirrored reflection of African-American life in Chicago because they clearly reflect African-American life at a certain level.

I'm sure Iyalosha Tanina Shongobumni would understand, and perhaps vote me an ash.

Perhaps the mirror is a small attempt, perhaps a somewhat tawdry attempt to clench our jaws on the images that we've had of ourselves, wherever. Or maybe its a grand look at

29

how we see ourselves beyond where we've been forced to be.

In any case, Bird oversees it all. We have to mention Bird because he will eventually become, like Coltrane, Ellington, Diz, Miles and a precious few others, an icon, and icons are reflections.

Backing up into the mirror.

They perch on the barstools, demurely sipping frothy drinks from tulip shaped, long stemmed glasses, glancing into the spotless mirrors behind the bar.

He sips his cognac, ties a bead onto her seductive eyelashes, pretends not to be attentive for a moment. A moment later their eyes lock as they lift frothy drink and cognac snifter simultaneously.

His lascivious off eye wink indicates that they were made for each other. She doesn't deny it with a licentious pout of her full lower lip.

Two stools to the left; matters are not going quite so smoothly. His eye punch is too aggressive, her beer is too flat, they are using the mirror for the wrong purposes.

The players in "The Game of the Mirrors" must be of age, minors are prohibited from playing.

Grade "A" players are role models of distinction. Some of them have actually reached the point of being able to use the mirrors telepathically.

One world renowned "mirror man" has been known to imprison selected Ladies in the mirror, to hold them in glamorous captivity for hours on end.

A sense of Africanity, of African-American aesthetics governs these behaviors; a certain, hip way of behaving ("don't talk to me, you're drunk"), a musical way of speaking ("she's got a loud voice"), a Hip if you buy the adjective.

The President's Lounge is packed, it's Friday night and the regulars are in the scene.

The graciously long bar lengthens our perspective from the door, a small sitting area back there under the silent screen T.V., the dance floor on the other side, adjacent to the other bars.

(It's many yards narrower than the Other Places' large bars, its satellite bars ("where you wanna sit, over there?"), numerous waitresses and cleverly distributed cocaine salespersons).

Middle aged jocks in full plumage prowl the space, tall glasses held at port arms, granting and receiving the low keyed versions of high fives.

Rakish hats, caps and berets fish for the glittering strobes, accentuate the conked eyes and pregnant glances.

Color coordinated brothers ("yellow on yellow in yellow, on Black") play out man—women games that are so intricately mapped that they sometimes forget the purpose for their cool activities.

High tech types who were once ghetto—brother man—stays, stare at the ensemble groups, romanticizing about other times, pleased to be on the scene but proud of not being a part of the scenery.

The African—colored—Negro—Black—African music pulls dancing bodies onto the dance floor where they play choreographic con games, fleece slick minds of kinetic energy and suck up on nebulous Africoid tits.

Chazz is symbolic of most of it. Brother Chazz, Brother Chazz, the symbol, representative, objective relief.

It might seem that Chazz was always there. He was there when Duke Ellington swung into town wearing a camel's hair, wrap around, collarless sports jacket,

Chazz was wearing a variation on the Theme, the following Thursday. He has always been stylish without seeming to be profile conscious. That really takes some effort in our community, a place where to style is, to profile, a notorious

31

trait.

Watched the brother many a night, in front of the President's Lounge, cop a stance in the parking lot of the Dating Game, take childish delight in the company of bonded brothers, look wisely innocent inside the Chicago Post Office, trade barbed shitticisms about town.

His frontal life seems to be a dance. How long has he been doing the latest dance? How many dances has he learned? known? been a part of? Will be a part of?

When Chazz dances, the place he is dancing in dances with him. Seen him dance with the President's Lounge many times, caused stiff asses at the bar to sway.

His dance succeeds because it is never interrupted by life; no sore loins, no fallen arches, blitzed out love affairs, concerns about bills to be paid or crazy international behavior. Brother Dances...

Chazz dances now, for himself—us, a sacred Dance to honor the moment. In some ways he is the Essential Dancer, a lot of his stuff traditional, some of it made up.

His dance forms the foundation, our foundation, for the interactions we have with each other: the pick 'n roll, the give 'n go, the spicy screen, the slip 'n slide...Michael Jordan, Chazz guards his position obviously, not jealously, and that keeps him on the top, year after year, keeps us going back 'n forth to Reeses' and the President's Lounge.

I'm going to have to stop what I'm doing right here and think about the Orisha in print...May 23, 1991, rainy day (Saturday), in Chicago.

I wasn't introduced to the idea of Ancestor worship, the way some fortunate people were. In some rare way the Orisha have always been part of my existence.

I can never remember when I wasn't appealing to one divine energy or another. Never could figure out why I had

32

to, what was happening in my head that forced me to make offerings, sacrifices.

It was never a question of God, but of gods of people who had developed a spiritual power that was strong enough for them to share it with anyone who made a very serious plea. Esu, Yemoya, Shango, Ogun, Oshun, Obatala', none of their names were familiar to me, growing up on the Westside of Chicago, but the energies that they personified were real to me, had meanings that I couldn't explain, still can't.

The Near West side was a beautiful place to come to grips with my ancestors, and the Orisha in an abstract sense they were all around me.

I was given the job of killing the chickens, of making the sacrifices for the Sunday feast. Nobody else wanted to do it. Or else this was something that enabled us to survive and thrive drove me into doing what had to be done.

Eleven fifty Wasburne was a shrine place. When I look back into it that's the only conclusion I can reach. Everyday, including Sunday, was a holy day, all of the people were Orisha believers (if not worshippers) and the connections were serious.

Every morning was started by Aunt Mary chanting, "Y'all ain't up yet, whatcha gon' do? Sleep all day?"

Iyalosha meant something to me before it meant something. This smallish (I thought she was six feet when I was enchanted by her) woman with the Mississippi-styled pompadour laid it all out for us.

She caused the fires to be lit, the ashes to be taken out, the babies to be born, love to be made, the chickens to be killed, the eggs to be laid, the gambling to begin, the atmosphere to be charged. Sister was stuff. She was in cahoots with shit that the rest of us shied away from. Why did she have fifteen dogs? (forty-five if the breeding season was on us).

I know, some of the orthodox people will say; she didn't come the regulation way, she didn't get initiated, she didn't serve, didn't do the rituals, didn't know the songs, couldn't've been right.

Who knows? They may be right. All I know is that she was an African spiritual guide for me; and those who paid attention.

No, she wasn't Cuban or Brazilian. She was a Mississippian, I'm sure, once proper investigations have been made, that the accident of birthing in that place will carry the same spiritual weight as a Gypsy singer being accredited in the caves of Cordoba, or a small town in Bahia.

Long winded way of saying that she knew her stuff.

But, let's not lay it all on Aunt Mary, she was an appendage.

My earliest understanding of The Religion swept Aunt Mary up into it, and also Uncle Percy, the Ascetic, her husband. Uncle Percy, the Gandhi-thin man who had once spent eleven years in the penitentiary for killing a man in a gambling dive.

Down there, underneath the street, they performed unnamed rituals the whole day long and never took a backward glance.

(Why did Aunt Mary really keep chickens in the pantry?)

The basement contained the elements for a serious African belief system and the so-called Christian Church (Baptist) two doors east of us affirmed the elements.

There was no doubt in my mind that the "church" was a cover for something deeper than the services that were announced on the billboard in front.

(Why was there a pot bellied stove in the front of the church? a bit off to the side, midway between the altar and the front row. Strange stove, it wasn't in anybody's way but you could burn yourself if things got out of hand.)

And why was the choir dressed in Elegba's colors?

And why did we have baptisms up there periodically, the initiates dressed in Obatala's color?

The preacher, the deacons, deaconesses (Uncle Percy was a deacon, Aunt Mary, a deaconess), the choir (four Mahalia Jackson's, five Ray Charles') and all the motions of what was happening inside the Sunrise Baptist Church went 'way 'round Christian stuff.

But that's something I picked up on later in life. I had to make pilgrimages to other belief sites before I reached some conclusions about to what I had been exposed.

The rhythms of the tambourine, the call and response of the singing, the fire glowing in the center of the "church," the seriousness of being "saved," of being put in touch with the Forces outside ourselves, Forces that often called people to clench their eyes and dance themselves away from this reality, cued me in.

No, I wasn't fooled for a minute. I knew that we were practicing The Religion, cleverly overlaid with just enough Christianity to make it "legit" for those who desperately needed assurances that their brainwashing had been successful. Or something.

I'd definitely be lying if I said that I understood, that I was clear about how our spirituality filtered through us, through our neighborhood.

What I did understand was that Washbourne was not integrated, it was African, except for the Jewish-colonialist-trader on one corner of Racine and Washbourne and the franchised Gentile supermarket on the other side.

I'm stressing the fact we weren't integrated because it meant, after business hours, we were left alone. Somehow this state of affairs seemed to decrease our dependence on white walls to bounce off our Blackness.

We could've been an African city within the city, and the

spirits that meant something were fed and allowed free expression.

People opened up with folk tales and went all the way down to haints.

Years later, after being immersed in this rich mix, I started checking out other belief systems and they reaffirmed what I had been raised in.

It was a bit like the trip that the racist anthropologists had taken, pretending to discover the origin of mankind in the caves of Europe, in the rice fields of China, everywhere but Africa.

The difference for me is that I didn't resist the idea of Africa. Somehow it seemed quite logical to me; if the origin of people happened in Africa, then that's where spirituality first occurred where the idea for creation myths happened, where the idea of The Religion was formed, had to be.

This realization enabled me to stop fighting with my Christian friends, all of those who were into the notion of monotheism.

I began to see how the depth of The Religion created the kind of spiritual strength needed to withstand the pressures of chattel slavery in the African Diaspora.

Everywhere I look in the world, I see African people who have migrated, immigrated, exported, imported. And I know that they/we are sustained and strengthened by the power of our Ancestors and the Orisha. Ase.

Momma was as typical of a certain kind of Chicagoan as they come. When I say "typical," I'm not talking about a stadium full of people, but rather a small roomful of people.

She came to Chicago from Helena, Arkansas, back in the '20's, when a lot of other Africans left the South. There isn't much I can say about that section because I didn't get to know her 'til 1937.

Small Kalahari woman (her nickname was "Lil' Bit"), filled with passion and vinegar. Momma (never mother, mommy or mom) was my introduction to the inner city, the guts lined with experiences impossible to come by anywhere else.

The primary level of things I had come to grips with dealt with her passion. Momma was a passionate woman. There were no half-nuts happening with her, she got the whole orgasm or somebody would be in serious trouble.

She ripped numerous shirts off of an assortment of would be cheaters ("I don't play that shit!") and played the fool for a couple of men. But it was all Chicago passion, in a way; she knew what she wanted and she knew what they wanted.

Sometimes she wanted spring, and you could tell; everything would be buds and sweetened water. The flavors would be darker after late June. If the man was going to be meaningful, we could be fairly sure that the first shirt she gave him would be burgundy or chicken hawk red.

But it wasn't only about shirts and aroused blood. There was a sense of Earth and Moon surrounding the woman, a kind of primeval happenin': she was the right size (how tall was Leakey's woman Lucy?) and the right shape (how many middle class kids can say they watched their "mother's" titties flop around until they were ten?) and she was deeply involved in African religious practices.

I can see it now, the superstitious mumbo jumbo that I never laughed at, mocked or thought funny. All of the incenses, powders, perfumes, candles, incantations, musical invocations, appeals to/for di-vine intervention ("O lawd! Help us!"), all of it.

Difficult shit. Why couldn't we just give up and not burn a candle for seven days? Why was it necessary to "clean" the house?

"Clean the house?" What house?

Take a fuckin' upturned kleenex box and scrub, wash and fumigate the motherfucker. What the hell was that about?

Yes, of course, I rejected some of the physical manifestations of her passion. Like being beaten about the head and shoulders by someone who seemed to be for the moment possessed by a demon or two.

But I loved moving from one side of town to the other, changing school often enough to prevent me from getting tied into knots by math tables or unpleasant encounters with the neighborhood thugs. They were there, waiting on me, but they had to be swift about doing what they wanted to do because any delay would find me gone, moved away.

We (my sister and I) were true nomads; a cardboard box, the clothes on our backs. Gypsies and Bedouin desert people in the National Geographic were role models, heroic figures to me, still are.

The nomadic thing for us wasn't a search for water, or fresh pasturage for the goats, it was usually a desperate attempt to find a room because we had been evicted. Yeah, loved the adventure of moving, hated being evicted. Being evicted meant that you came home from school (about eighteen of them) and the lady next door would have a note telling you where the cardboard boxes had been re-routed.

"Lil' Bit" knew her world. She didn't know downtown because there wasn't a large number of Black people living downtown. Her world was the Southside ghetto, the Westside ghetto and the Northside ghetto.

She knew the people in her world, a master ghetto psychologist. I noticed that she did several things upon arrival at a new den, uh place. She immediately got into her neighbors, if she didn't already know them.

She would determine, number one, who was likely to have

some money to loan her. Number two, if there was a nice middle aged woman she could trust her children with, if she had to make an extended run.

Beyond that it was a matter of getting the low down on everybody's business. I guess it was her way of securing her place in the scheme of things, no matter how brief the time frame was going to be.

The information that she treasured would include the whereabouts of the nearest gambling scene. It wasn't difficult to find the gambling room.

In most of the broken down buildings we lived in somebody would have a pair of dice, a deck of cards or some other way to mess off some money.

If she couldn't find the game, she'd invent one. I can close my eyes for a second and picture the sight of the lady kneeling on the edge of a rough blanket, surrounded by a grizzled collection of hard edged ex-cons, men with keloid knife slashes across their faces, women who gave the impression of being from the Stone Age.

She won and lost, but the deeper impression for me was her involvement in the game, the opportunity to take a chance.

If you're going to be alive, she seemed to be saying, you must gamble.

She was an artist of life, surviving but never thriving for longer than it took to spend the "relief" check. She was also another kind of artist, a person who decorated her environment.

It never took longer than a few minutes for her to decide where a picture she clipped from the magazine should be pasted up, where the strips of paper should be strung from which length of overhead pipes.

It was these little attentions to aesthetics, in a sense, that made life bearable. Her artistic senses, like her cooking was compounded by emergencies.

Never knew anyone who could transform scraps of stuff into edibles as well as she could. Perhaps, if any producer ever bought the idea, the show could be called "the Ghetto Gourmet."

I've joked about her cooking on other pages, years after I had passed the stage of damned near starving. I can't joke now, looking back at skillets and pots that were filled with stuff that gave us the courage to face winter ravaged Chicago mornings.

Or make it through a day that would've been empty, had it not been for her ability to transform an onion and a wedge of cornbread into a bowl of Mexican chili, a fried chicken breast, a bowl of meatballs and spaghetti or whatever a fertile imagination wanted to pretend the fried cornbread and onion dish called "kush" was.

The Lady's entrepreneurship was much less successful than her way with scraps of scraps, "Lil Bit," the wine seller. I can still smell the babyshit-sour odor of a dedicated cheap wine drinkers breath in my face.

What was it? Some crazy law that said you couldn't buy wine from the local bodega until twelve o'clock on Sunday morning, time enough for the people who had the shakes to be shaking into spasms.

She decided to take up the slack by buying a case of red and white port on Saturday and re-selling it on Sunday morning.

The idea was to make a dime off each bottle ($0.50 per pint). It never happened. Some shakers got it for $0.40, some for $0.30, many for nothing at all.

Maybe the idea behind the whole get rich scheme was simply to serve the community wine when they needed it. In any case, profit was not the motive with her that it was with some people.

What she lost on wine sales she made up for it with her emotional investments, her love thang. My Momma was a lover.

She loved a variety of men, tall, short, small, large, thin, fat, bald, non-bald, smart, dumb. She loved my father, who was not too tall or too short, but very dark, smart and handsome.

They had a childish attraction that produced two children and then a deep romance that gave birth to a serious friendship, years after the midday brawls and midnight love feasts.

I'm 99% certain that Daddy was her first love. How many men could she have loved before getting married and pregnant at 16?

The fact that they had two children to raise before they were twenty years old was never a drag for them. Momma was the primary keeper of the kids but we were quite well behaved and considered "cute," which made it easier for her to stash us (together or separately) with responsible friends.

If I had been a "Love Detective" I would've had enough evidence to convict both of them to eternal damnation. I was always running into Momma (most often Daddy) with someone, obviously off to do some sort of adulterous stuff.

I don't know if they busted each other on occasion, but my guess is that they did. And when they did, there was hell to pay.

They had wall to wall lovers and didn't seem to care a lot about who knew it. Momma thrived on complex relationships with simple men. Daddy was the other way, he loved simple relationships with complex women.

They were hot when they were hot and never cooled down until she died and he was killed.

I didn't know that they were bonafide writers until they

41

were both gone. It dawned on me, checking out a collection of letters he had written her from prison. I wasn't privileged to read her replies.

However, I was exposed to many of her creative ideas on paper whenever she had to write a can't miss begging note to somebody in the building, or invent an artful reason for keeping me from school.

I always feel that she is nourishing me whenever I come back to Chicago, to walk the familiar streets and search for faces that I once knew in other forms.

I always feel her presence here and everywhere.

The Blues

We are re-exposed to them on the PBS channels across the country, in Chicago its WTTW. They are a bunch of Black guys sitting at pianos and entrenched guitar stools, plunking, strumming and singing their hearts out.

It isn't really singing, really. It's more like someone using their voices to reach back into a different emotional frame of reference.

These grizzled old African men dig down into themselves in front of mostly white audiences, mostly younger types who can afford to go slumming in the latest yuppie blues havens.

Shamefully, the young African people have turned their backs on these men, on this music, on their ancestors. We can only pray that they will wake up one day and realize what the so-called Blues means.

A Night at the Sutherland

The Sutherland Hotel is/was (if it hasn't been destroyed) located at 47th and Drexel Blvd., northeast corner and at one time, it had the hippest jazz club in the city in the premises.

This, mind you, was during the London House period, the Brownshoe in Old Towne, the Blue Note, the Regal Theatre and a whole collection of lesser known spots (The Flamingo Lounge, McKies, the Pershing Hotel, the C and C Lounge, places where music was played live and APPRECIATED.

The Sutherland Lounge in the Sutherland Hotel was a leader. Never knew who owned the place, didn't know what the inside deals were, or why, but it was the place to go and check Art Blakey out, Ahmad Jamal, Lou Donaldson, Diz, Bird would've played there if they had lived long enough.

Miles Davis was there the night my friend Raoul decided to take this white girl he had blundered into. At the time, when Miles tripped into the Sutherland he came to play, not to shuck 'n jive.

The audience had a lot to do with it, they wouldn't allow him the space to play with them, he had to play for them or else people would start talking directly to him, on stage, and not heckle...

Marvelous horse shoe shaped stage up there behind the bar. The tables were something else, but the waitresses were fairly cool and didn't try to coerce you into ignoring the music.

Miles Davis, a super hip audience, Raoul and the white girl. She was a good looking motherfucker, that was something we all acknowledged. A real white girl, not a frizzy hair Sephardic from the Westside, but a real tall Scandinavian type from the far Northside.

Sherman, one of our least polite types had openly quizzed Raoul about Margreta.

"How the fuck did you cut into a White Bitch like that, man?"

He patiently explained; "I pulled her at Oak Street Beach, a place you unadventurous motherfuckers wouldn't even think about going to."

Raoul was right. But Raoul thought he was right about most things. His name was really Richard but he thought Raoul was more like him than Richard.

"Fuck a Richard! I ain't into nothing that a Richard would be into, I'm into being Raoul."

And so, with no arguments from us, he became Raoul. He wore berets a lot, smoked his herb in a cigarette holder, idolized Black women "ain't nothin' on Earth as beautiful as a Black women! with that butter on the hips, them neat little waistlines, them pretty tidies and those gorgeous lips 'n shit— but he dated white women as often as he could.

He viciously denied any preference for white over black.

"Fuck y'all! It ain't about that, it's about freedom of choice 'n what we got in common."

He didn't want to hear that some sister his age (24) could be into Miles.

"No, sisters wanna listen to the Ravens, or the Shirelees 'n shit like that. It's them white broads that's into our music."

So, thusly it came to pass that Richard, alias Raoul, would wind up in the Sutherland Lounge on a gorgeous-summer Friday night with a white woman named Margreta Lundgren.

We were all there that night, even Sweet Peter Deeder, giving his' hoes a rare rest period. Us younger ones, who didn't have grand theft incomes, had sold, stole, begged and borrowed to meet the entrance fee and two drinks per set minimum.

Miles, Philly Joe, Paul Chambers, Coltrane, Cannonball and Wynton Kelly were going to play together for the weekend at the Sutherland Lounge and the aficionado had to make the pilgrimage.

It wasn't much of a problem for Raoul to be there, Miss Lundgren made certain of that.

"You don't have to worry too much about money when you hanging out with these white broads, they get allowances 'n shit."

If the truth means anything we were somewhat envious of Raoul. He was going to be able to sit at a choice table and buy as many gin 'n tonics as Miss Lundgren could afford.

Four of us were positioned three tables away from him and his blonde benefactress. Nice thing about the Sutherland, you really couldn't really get a bad seat, it was purely a matter of looking up at the stage.

Raoul, trying to maintain his community-love image, cast smirks and sly smiles at us from time to time. We were cool.

The Lady seemed to be in a Disneyland state, her head swiveled around flinging her golden locks this way 'n that, as she chucked Roaul under the chin and tried to riffle her hand through his conk.

Enviously we watched them go thru two gin 'n tonics before the lights were dimmed.

Be'Be leaned across the table and whispered, "Damn! That Bitch must be richer than Carnation cream."

We nodded in agreement.

I pinned them onto my little mental butterfly wall and tried to get a fix on what made them a couple, what kind of chemistry was happening.

Like I said earlier, it was an acknowledged fact that she was a good looking motherfucker. She was a white good looking woman, not an imitation Black woman or anything like that.

What I'm trying to say is that comparisons between different kinds of people just won't work. Her blue eyes, blonde hair and pale-freckly skin could only have come from generations of blue eyed, blonde haired, pale freckly people.

She did have a wonderful set of milk jugs on her, though.

The musicians almost do a little dance tripping up the steps to the stage. Never witnessed the Sutherland Lounge audience go into that obligatory pre-set applause bullshit.

They had to give it to us fresh every time. The tension was dark textured. Everybody was on stage but Miles.

"Where is that Little evil Black Motherfucker?" One of the players spoke loud enough for the in joke to be heard.

Lundgren's head snapped around as though she had been slapped, and scowled in the direction of the hipster.

Raoul patted her lightly on a freckly arm and whispered something mollifying in her silky earlobe.

It was evident that she didn't relate to affectionate profanity and that she was on her way to being "white-drunk" as Beau Felt defined it.

"What's being 'white drunk?'" Well, there's a bunch of ways to define it. I think it would be better to describe the behaviors and let you reach your own definition. Or definitions.

Number one, it doesn't take a lot of anything to ring the "white drunk" bell. I was in the Army with dudes who would get fucked up on that 3.2 beer from the PX and start howling like wolves 'n beatin' each other in the head with chairs.

Real examples of primitive "white-drunk" shit, the woman seem to go into a neurotic mode when they get "white

47

drunk." They break into tears and start giving up the story of their miserable lives. In addition, they usually want to bring some kind of sexual garbage onto the scene.

You know, shit like, would you let my husband peek thru the screen at us if you fuck me? Shit like that.

There're so many variations of the "white drunk" that it would be impossible to give a rock hard definition. Strangely, in my lifetime, I've only seen two Black people go "white drunk" one of them was a brother who had fallen in love with country and western music and hated himself because he loved the Confederate Flag.

The other was a sister who had graduated from an exclusive all white girl's school where it was popular to be as fucked up as possible, the motto of the school could've been—"I don't know where my fucking head is"—pronounced in that super clipped way that folks speak after they've gone to school too long and don't know shit about life.

Beau Felt was right on it, we winked at each other from across our watery drinks, Miss Lundgren was going into a "white drunk" mode.

She ignored Miles Davis' appearance on stage as she plunged her glistening red tongue into Raouls ear and draped her right arm around his neck in a boa constrictor embrace.

Raoul was trying to be cool because he knew we were checking him out, but he was beginning to express a whole new body language of discomfort.

Miles had blasted open with a toe tapper, I forget what the tune was, maybe it was "Night n' Tunisia" or something. Mostly what I remembered was Philly Joe Jones sticks twirling around from drum to drum like a dervish.

Everybody got a piece; Paul Chambers locked into some kind of Hindo rhythm, I don't know what that shit was he was playing. 'Trane got fired up and damned near had to be prodded away from the mike, and it was pretty much the

48

same with Cannonball and Wynton Kelly.

They put the pot on and righteously cooked for about thirty hard minutes; it went from hard bop to salsa tinged fringes to something that sounded like Senegalese blues and then back to bop.

During the course of the first number, the lady made two exhibitionistic trips to powder her nose. How could you go pee when Coltrane was pouring musical money in your ear?

Miles sneered in her direction as she bumped and ground her way thru the audience. The consensus was that Raoul would be lucky to get past Miles Davis' "Funny Valentine."

The second time she tripped thru to be seen, Raoul hunchbacked to our table and said, "Order what you want, I'll put it on our check."

All four of us stared as skeptically as we could stare at him.

"You sure its gon' be cool man?" Hawk asked him, "I mean we don't wanna get embarrassed up in here."

"It's cool," he answered with a sigh, and pulled out four C notes.

"Thanks, Raoul, you a beautiful cat, man," Brother Be'Be' whispered to him.

"Whooh, here she comes," he whispered in a panic and scuttled back to their table.

The music was already happenin', but now, with no bar bill to worry about, it became delicious.

We signalled to the waitress for another round, she was already hip to the scene and accepted our thanks, "I know, its on his tab," with a gracious smile.

As we all know, or remember, Miles never announced his pieces, but by the time he got to "Green Dolphin Street" the house was levitating with good jazz vibes, except for Margreta Lundgren. She was "white drunk."

"Well just who is this guy anyway, Raoul that he doesn't tell you what he's playing. How 'bout a lil' kiss for baby

49

hmmmmm?''

She didn't know who Miles Davis was, or Philly Joe, or 'Trane or Cannonball or Kelly! That was obviously bad enough but now she was beginning to slur a lot and talk loud.

The back of Raoul's conk began to look like a latter day jheri curl dripping. If he had been a white man his neck would've been as red as a buzzard's beak after the kill.

Have to give it to the brother, he hung in there. When her outburst got too ebullient—''how 'bout two more over here?!''—he would sorta clamp his hand around he upper arm and lean over and whisper real urgently into her ear.

I couldn't hear what he was saying to her but it would cool her out for a few minutes and then she'd hit it again.

''Raoul''

''Yeah, what?''

''Let's dance.''

All of the people near enough to hear the exchange looked at each other in amazement. Had anybody ever thought of dancing in the Sutherland, to Miles playing ''All Blues''?

''Uhh, we can't dance up in here, Margreta.''

''Why not?''

The words came like gravelly thunderclaps from the top of a tall mountain: ''Shut up, Bitch!''

Miles Davis had spoken. Raoul slid six inches lower in his seat as the white girl pulled herself into a fetal knot in her chair, her hands clutched to her ears, her blue eyes rolling from side to side like loose marbles.

I think it was the first time that evening that she had actually paid any attention to the stage, and her reaction was terror and fear. God had called her a Bitch.

Mercifully the set ended, Raoul couldn't seem to figure out a way to hold his head low enough, but Miss Lindgren, having recovered somewhat had gotten a second wind.

''Oooh Raoul! isn't it exciting?!''

50

The collection of jazz lovers applauded long and hard. Miles ignored it, of course, and made a quick exit. The other players however, made gracious bows before they left the stage.

We signalled for another round. The lights were up and everybody was checking everybody out, the way they used to do at the Sutherland. It would've been impossible not to see this large boned Black man with all these muscles stroll thru the aisles towards Raoul's table.

Real big Black man with a Michael Jordan hair cut and a beautifully cut tuxedo on his back.

He stood in front of Raoul's table like an ebony statue for a full quiet minute. When he spoke his voice had the sound of black velvet.

"The management requests that the two of you not attend the second set. Furthermore, the management requests, that the two of you not come to the Sutherland Lounge ever again."

I'm not certain, but I thought I saw the glisten of a tear well up in the corner of Raoul's eyes.

He was being barred from the Sutherland, he was being exiled from one of the jazz heavens in Chicago.

Hawk, a quick thinker, immediately sized up the situation and frantically signalled for our waitress.

"Uhh look, uhh, what's your name?"

"Rose."

"Rose, we want to save you the trouble of running back 'n forth during the next set, you think you could bring each of us four drinks each on Raoul."

"No problem."

Raoul, poor brother, I don't even think he paid much attention to the tab. He had been barred from the Sutherland.

He tried to slink past our table but we wouldn't let him, each of us solemnly shook his hand and tried to say something

51

sympathetic.

"Well, Homes, sorry you gon' miss the second set, you know that's when it really gets loose."

He nodded and slunk on out behind Miss Lundgren, who was ranting and raving about discrimination and shit.

"I mean, I can't believe it! After all you people have been thru, Raoul, how can they discriminate against other people? They're picking on us because we're a mixed couple, right?"

We settled back for the second set which of course, was 110 degrees hotter than the first set. During one climatic run Hawk, actually screamed. It wasn't the music that made him do it, however, he thought his lit cigarette had wedged between his legs.

And too soon it was over, we stumbled out onto the blue streaked streets of the southside and wandered until we found out way home, loaded to the gills.

Didn't see and couldn't find Raoul for days.

"Hey man, when you seen Raoul?"

"I ain't seen him since that night at the Sutherland."

"He's probably hanging up North." Of course, we had all agreed not to anything about the scene at the Sutherland, but it wasn't necessary.

In that telepathic way that news is transmitted on the Southside (and the Westside, and wherever Black people live) everybody seemed to know already.

When I finally ran into Raoul, about three months later, he seemed like a different person.

"Raoul, what it is brother? Where you been keeping yourself?"

"Call me Richard, man, my real name is Richard."

We kicked it around for awhile, even strolled over to the Place for a taste, but the Sutherland and Miss Lundgren never came up in our conversation.

Years later, back in Chicago on an annual visit, I ran into

Richard again. We were both older, ten pounds heavier, grey on the top and bottom, relatively successful you might say.

We popped into the President's Lounge for a cognac, made our way into the Other Place (it was a Saturday night and wound up in a quiet little bar on Cottage Grove and Marquette Road.

"Richard, something I've wanted to ask you for years,"

"I know, about me 'n the white girl, right?"

"Yeah, whatever happened?"

"Well, you know we had to split up behind some crazy shit like that. Imagine, being barred from the Sutherland. But you see what happened to them? The fucking place went bankrupt and closed."

After all these years I could see bitterness in the down curled corners of his mouth.

We finished off the evening with him showing me pictures of his beautiful Ethiopian wife and four teenaged children.

"I met her in England, a conference."

We parted company on a mellow note after promising each other we'd keep in touch, Richard-Raoul was a powerful reminder of nights at the Sutherland Lounge.

Wonder what happened to the white girl?

Dances

Africans in Chicago are always dancing. Black children dance while waiting for the stop light to change from red to green and then they dance across the street, inventing unique little stutter steps and dips.

Middle aged brothers and sisters do a dance-walk, feeding on inner-ear music. The silky dip and postured pause demand a graceful splay of the feet, an artful slackness of the hip, it could be called ballet.

Older men, women go to nightclubs, where they dance with each other, and others years younger. They do dances that some of them have been doing since the Twenties. And they're still popular under other names.

The original types have their special steps, stuff that they've worked out over the years. The followers maintain the bass rhythms, the soft back upon which the thing is carried.

In any case, the dancing goes on, even when it sounds like the music has stopped....

The Projects

Some of the gratest dancers in Chicago, in the world, live in the projects.

"Billie Holiday" lives on the 10th floor of one of the sandwiched boxes of the Robert Taylor Homes. "Billie" is twelve years old and has been singing all her life. She sings from the time she wakes up 'til she goes to bed.

She sings commercials, popular songs, raps, whatever passes thru her head, but her personal preference is for Billie Holiday.

"I don't really know what it was about Billie Holiday that grabbed me."

"Billie" sits at the corner of an ancient dinette table, her pregnant belly wedged between her and the table. From time to time she stares pensively down in to the common courtyard shared by all the inmates.

Snatches of "Stormy Monday," "Don't Explain" and "Strange Fruit" spill out of her as naturally as the story of her life.

"My grandmother lived in the projects. It's kinda hard to believe that any old person could live in the projects."

"Billie" is lovely, no doubt in anybody's mind about that. The young man (28 yrs old) who got her in a family way doesn't think she is quite as beautiful as she once was, however.

"Hey, don't get me wrong, I still think "Billie" is

something special, but now, since she done messed up 'n got pregnant 'n shit, she seems to have changed a lot. You know what I mean? Shes not as much fun as she used to be.''

"No, I don't remember my father, really. He like a shadow in my life.''

The grizzled old timers pop into the "Holiday" apartment on the weekends (which are apt to start on Thursday), wine, beer, gin and whisky bottles held at port arms, loaded, thirsty for the sound of "Billiers" renditions of Billie's music.

"It's mostly the older people who want to hear me sing Billie Holiday's music. The younger people, my friends, they ain't into it, they say its too slow 'n draggy.''

She sits at the dinette table, her hands folded like a shy school girl, and sings,'' them thats got shall get, them thats not shall lose, so the Bible says, and it still is news.

"Momma may have, Poppa may have, but God bess the child thats got his own . . .''

"Thats her, baby, thats really her. You got Billie in your souls.''

Sometimes they leave a few bills in the dish on the table, some offer her a drink.

"No thank you, it ain't good for the baby.''

"Yeah, it is something, ain't it? Ain't nobody on either side of our family can carry a tune in a bucket, and now she comes along.''

Robert Taylor acrobats, an esoteric breed for whom the term "daring" is the least descriptive of their activities, swing from one tall building to the other, unconcerned about falling.

They don't hear "Billie" or care about Billie, their only concern is with the width of the line and whether or not it will carry them to the transfer point of wires; the wire of powdered coke to the crystal from called crack.

The chemists on the 8th floor, protected by a belligerent

army of drug sapped look outs, mix and sample the latest dream stuff, euphemistically entitled, "happy shit."

Boys and girls, some of them acting as look outs for the makers of "happy shit," others into more legitimate forms of acting, form an effervescent base in the projects.

They are everywhere; posturing preening, rehearsing, reciting their lines, trying out new versions of old stories on each other.

"Yo' momma so fat she cain't even walk."

"Yeah, well yo' momma so ugly she can't even catch a cold."

Some days, in the muggy heat of a Chicago summer, they seem like candy stoked dervishes, whirling from one small theatre in the round to the next small theatre in the round.

The whole project is a stage and they are the actors on it. Fifteen years olds pretend to be thirty, in order to join the gang and receive the protection that being in a gang grants the bad actors.

Robin Hoods do not take from the rich (in the Projects) and give to the poor. They take from the poor and keep it.

Writers are a dime a dozen on these grounds, they write with their lips, they are lipwriters, storyfinders, as in "finders keepers, losers weepers."

They blend into the mix of poets, rappers, space agents, hypnotists, painters and lawyers, all elements of this volatile situation called the Projects.

The projects were designed to oppress Black people in Chicago. Some dishonest believers lie and say, "The projects were created to give the low income people an opportunity to have a decent place to live."

The outrageous lie that acted as the catalyst for the development of the projects still earns a few innocents, but it doesn't wash well with the hip and the really intelligent.

The projects are civilian peniteniaries, the inmates are

primarily women with children (a clever ordinance mandated the absence of men, fathers), the warden (the City) and a set of elaborately designed social circumstances to keep a tight rein on the beast that rages within.

The projects are ugly and incur the animosity of any sensitive person who is forced to live there. The sensitive person, enraged by the architectural nightmare that stacks him/her layer upon layer, surrounded by meshed wire and designs that mock his/her sense of African aesthetics will, at the first opportunity, attempt to beautify, crucify, mutilate, draw or graffitize on the brutal walls around them.

All of the laboratory experiments that "ethics" prevent the morally conscious from carrying out in the sterile labs of the country, are routinely conducted in the projects.

Project: What is the simple effect of caging ten-thousand human beings layer upon layer within structures that create hate for one's surroundings?

Project: How long does it take to create anti-social behavior within artifically divided groups (gangs)?

Project: If men, fathers, are denied the traditional role of men, fathers, how will that effect the children?

Project: Are African-Americans capable of overcoming generations of life in the projects?

If African-Americans are walled off, given the worse food possible, inferior educations, exceptionally negative images of themselves and excessive amounts of sugar, what will happen?

Drug experimentation is relentless, sustained and premeditated. We can be certain that most of the latest chemically based drugs are given their first tryout in the projects.

The most elaborately developed dances are reserved for the beaurocracy. Who can say when that particular time step was first performed to dazzle the social workers? Or why

58

that ice cold shimmy was used to skirt the issue of man-loneliness on the application that boldly asks, "Are you now, or have you ever been...?"

Most of the dances are tightly structured, with an emphasis on economy of motion. No one can afford to use more energy than necessary. And the names are definitely indications of what they are meant to express.

The latest dance is called, "The project freedom step." Some people say it resembles the Electric Slide....

Hyde Park Lives! Now 'n Then

Some say Hyde Park is dead, the Bohemian element washed up, the groove set adrift. A surface look might encourage that brand of thinking; people dash from the bank to the mall, from the mall, to the Co-Op, from there to the latest sale.

"It ain't nothing like it used to be."

Prideless Black men in kente cloth caps beg on corners where brothers and sisters once proclaimed their divinity to any white person available.

Pale grey types shuffle past in their Earth Day sandals, briefcases filled with briefs, or directions for the latest bomb.

A facade lingers, however. The exhibitionists chess players and espresso cafe' aficionados do their best to call on an earlier time, but it doesn't really work.

It worked when we went to the Hyde Park Theatre for an afternoon of communion with "A Picasso Documentary," or the latest Bergman movie (which let everybody out of the dark brooding and filled as with Swedish angst, even the Black people) or the latest French farce.

French farces were the thing at the Hyde Park.

Smallish, arty theatre, no frills, usually overflowing with University of Chicago students, student-atmosphere parasites and "mixed" couples who made the pilgrimage in order to escape the oppression of their own narrow minded neighborhoods.

The Hyde Park was as escapist as could be. I remember a young white kid (probably the ten year old son of a bearded graduate student) who seemed to be the personification of the Hyde Park romantic, in attendance for the next to last showing of Jose' Ferrer's "Cyrano de Bergerac."

The place wasn't overflowing on this particular evening (Sartre, Camus, and Jean Genet were batting 1-2-3 at the time) and the focus of attention gradually settled on this young guy.

In today's terms he would obviously be considered a nerd, or one of those other frightening terms ordinary people coin for people who believe in their brains.

Opaque horn rimmed glasses, freckles that glowed in the heat of the black and white reflections, a Dennis the Menace hair cut and slightly bucked teeth.

He ooohhed and aaahhed at the speeches Cyrano put into the handsome dummy's mouth for transmission to Roxanne's silky ears.

He grunted with the effort to sword fight fifteen of the villainous beasts who threatened the de Bergerac probicis. He sighed, he called out to friends and foes, he suffered with Cyrano de Bergerac, he moaned at the dis-functioning of a fate that would stick such a beak on a man.

And at the end of the film he stood and applauded. We couldn't join him because the film hadn't touched us the way it had touched him, and we would've been guilty of patronizing him if our applause wasn't as sincere and honest as his.

The memory of faces shattered by the little guy's lack of cynicism played on my head, for days.

A romantic time, that's what a lot of it was about, romance. We romanced everywhere possible. It was possible (the Sixties, Pre-AIDS) to spend the day on the Point (57th Street jut of rocks on the lake front) and have a romance.

As a matter of fact it was a prime place for romance. We went in search of women. And vice versa. And it helped matters considerably if the man was Black and the woman was other than Black.

Interracialism meant something concrete (and romantic). The Black man who prowled the Point in pursuit of white romance wasn't talked about as bitterly as he would be in later years.

The urge to integrate had gripped some sisters in a grip so feverish that they granted soft core approval to Black man/White woman hook-ups.

"I mean, c'mon, why should I get upset? Some of my best girlfriends are white."

Things changed, of course, when the statistics began to show that more and more Black women were having fewer chances to mate with Black men. Hmmmmmmmm...

But, before the evil influences of reality and date-less Saturdays began to create ill will, "romance" flourished.

Jimmy's tavern on 55th Street was the place for liaisons, romances and gin 'n tonics (or pitchers of beer if you were a "poor student").

The music (Mozart, the MJQ or possibly Pete Seeger) was played on a great system, the weekend crowd was filled with strange ideas (Being and Nothingness was big) and if you had missed her on the Point, you could quite likely find her in Jimmy's.

The University of Chicago co-ed and that electric collection of significant other women who guzzled and ginned their off study times were rare studies in behavior.

The African-American sisters (the "radicals" wanted to be called Black) flounced through, dressed as ethnically as they knew how, usually a cross get up between a Peruvian poncho and some sort of gauzy Indian pajama pants, no one seems to have heard of kente at the time.

They mastered a way of talking that kept their teeth clenched and smiling, and their full lips semi-stationary. They were usually in the company of, or searching for a bearded white guy with visible signs of eye strain.

The brothers came for the white girls and there were several distinct types from which to choose. The "romantics" dominated, of course, and whenever possible they would try to dig down into the woodpile as far as possible. They went lock, stock and panties to the first African (from Africa) to show his mug.

The "defiant" ones were usually Jewish, Italian, Irish, German, Polish or possibly a mixture of all of the above. They were there to defy their parents, their prejudiced heritages, their ethnicities.

Orgies were in. Some people felt that group love was the best love.

"I mean, lets face it, man, this one-on-one stuff isn't going to do anything but lead to attachment."

"The Europeans" were those twenty-twenty one year olds who had biked around Europe drinking wine and fucking an occasional Spaniard, or Greek. Someone whose swarthiness was just the right preparation for a darker taste of the homegrown product.

And finally, the "high wire walkers," the "trapeze artists." They were usually third/fourth generation Americans from small towns where nothing had ever happened, and now they were in Chicago, the big city, and they wanted to let it rip.

"The high wire walkers," "the trapeze artists" usually drank more wine and smoked more of the mild marijuana than the others, often proclaiming their love for mankind, "I don't pay any attention to a person's color." And frequently announced, "I don't know where my head is, I really don't."

The release of new sexual information might find her head between the brother's thighs. Or the brother's head between her thighs, further complicating the mental location of her head.

Jimmy's was the full blown tree, the roots rested firmly in the sweating soil of the Hyde Park party.

The Hyde Park party, when orchestrated by the best of the Hyde Park party givers, was a definitive study in mixtures.

Four-five darks, a brown or two, a yellow, if one could be found without a heavy accent, several frizzy haired "trapeze artists," four Pete Seeger types (preferably one with a guitar) and an assortment of beards and sandals.

The mixture was stirred vigorously with liberal application of cheap wine (maybe an upper or two, if it were really "live") and coarse admonishments to "go! go! go! go! man! go!"

It was always Spring in Chicago for the Hyde Park Party, the air flecked with new buds and the hint of fragrant lake smells everywhere.

The typical party featured long winded conversations that skirted race; racial discussions were considered beneath the notice of authentic Hyde Park party people. We were all integrated, living in harmony and there was no need to shatter any bubbles by suggesting that any other illusion was viable.

This was the attitude carefully maintained by the white folks, in any case. Of course, there were a number of Black people who agreed with this warped notion, which was their philosophical justification for being a part of the scene.

The parties usually ended at twelve midnight or at dawn. It was just about like that, a kind of Cinderella syndrome or devil may care attitude.

No matter whether it was midnight or the following dawn, we could be certain that a few drunken arguments had happened a few surreptitious kisses exchanged, perhaps a quickie in a back bedroom (no herpes heard of, AIDS non existent, only the possibility of claps), lots of sentimental behavior between Bob Dylan and Miles Davis "Kind of Blue."

And finally it would be over 'til next time. If the party animal in the Hyde Parker hadn't been soothed by the cheap wine and the low grade pot, there was always the Near Northside.

The Near Northside was a more glamorous form of Bohemia than Hyde Park, and more expensive to prowl in.

The Near Northside was gorgeous bodies on Oak Street beach (prejudiced whites seeking tanned salvation), the College of Complexes, Hail Professor Corey; Figaros, Mr. Kellys, the Gate of Horn, the Brownshoe, the Rush street—Division scene.

It was always midnight and beyond when we tripped past Buckingham fountain, on the way to that hip little waffle joint where the middle echelon Near Northsiders and assorted folks from the fast tracks made their last stand of the night.

We went with women, usually, sisters of the night, people who could relate to the pace and wouldn't bloat up on Belgian waffles at 3 a.m.

Heads caked with the memory of the party, half-dazed from alcoholic residuals, we munched our waffles and spied on the scene.

The people who wandered in were a cross section of white night life in Chicago; Mafiosa, Dresden China call girls on R and R, fantastic Afro-pimps in Black transvestite of all kinds, gay foreigners whispering forbidden languages, con men on a spree, wandering shepherds, Negroes seeking the proximity of thrillin' white flesh, night dwellers.

And finally, dawn streaking the Lake Front, we'd return to the Southside.

"What about this thing on Saturday, man?"

"The one where they're supposed to be doin' poetry 'n shit?"

"Yeahh, that one."

"Might be interesting."

"Yeah, might be. I'll check with you later in the week."

Back to the Roots

Riga Lieutskas strolled north on State Street, her violin case tucked under her arm, pausing to peer into the well stocked windows of the downtown stores.

America was so rich, had so many beautiful things, so much. Riga stared at her reflection in one of the windows. She felt as differently as she looked, after six months in Chicago, America.

I was heavier in Lithuania, she thought, and smiled at the new Riga, the "American" Riga. A lush breeze gently swept the street, lulling her into a kind of spring time revery.

June 1991, she noted on a calendar inside a shop window.

June 1991, no political activities in the streets, no upheaval, no secret meetings, none of the thousands of problems that made Lithuania a place under the fist of the Russians' History.

People smiled at her, a beautiful young woman with intense grey eyes, simply dressed in a black skirt and an embroidered Lithuanian blouse.

Her parents had joked with her about what would happen when she got to America.

Her father made the grim forecast: "You will become an 'American in' six months, if you're not careful. I've seen it happen. Right after the war when a number of people were allowed out, many of them returned barely able to speak proper Lithuanian."

He was always joking like that, until it was actual time for her to leave.

"Riga, we know that you will never forget who you are, where your home is, who we are."

They sent her to America as though she were on a mission.

Her paternal grandparents had immigrated to the United States after Stalin's death and were offering their granddaughter sponsorship.

Her mother had often given her long winded monologues about Anton and Vilma Lieutskas.

"They were always doing things ahead of time. If there was money to be made, we could be certain that Anton and Vilma would put themselves in a position to make it. If there was the possibility of squeezing through an opening no smaller than this—they would do it.

Even if my family hadn't been killed in the War, they would never have gone to America. A trip to Vilnius was a big thing for them. But not your grandma and grandpa, they saw the opening and they ran thru it into a better life in America. Thank God they made it.

You must do your best for them, because they are offering you a rare opportunity to study, to become a great violinist. You must work very hard, Riga, you must prove that the money they are spending on you is well spent."

Riga Lieutskas clenched her fists and put more purpose into her step. After two hours of practice with Professor Bronte downtown, she was on her way home for three more hours in the basement of the Lieutskas home in northwestern Chicago.

Professor Bronte was not one to offer extravagant praise or raise false expectations but he had assured her, "Riga, my dear, I think you are ready now for concert work, I will speak with someone in my agent's office about you."

She felt exhilarated, alive for the first time in a way she

hadn't been before. Playing the violin was a pleasure, learning music was something of a chore but it was all part of the process.

"The musical scores, my dear, are the bullets for your weapon." Chicago was a vibrant place, the people colorful and direct.

No one made fun of her accent, or the hesitant way she spoke English. English was not a big problem, she had studied it from the first grade in grammar school. The problems she had, had to do with the variety of ways people spoke the language.

None of her textbooks or teachers had prepared her to understand the accent/dialects of Spanish speaking—Chinese—Polish—African—American speech, and others too obscure for her to figure.

English wandered around inside the mouths of people whose native languages were so differently pronounced that they, in effect were creating a different language each time they spoke English.

Like me, she whispered to herself, and smiled...

The train moved briskly from station to station, the conductor monotoning instructions—"No radio playing, excessive noise or drinking of alcohol. Next stop..."

She was back in her "neck of the woods," someone had called it. There were enough signs in Lithuanian to let everybody know that this was a predominantly Lithuanian neighborhood.

She walked the three blocks to her grandparents home, her mind on the new technique Professor Bronte had demonstrated.

Yusef Malik glared at the yuppie couple at table number three as he performed his solo.

Fuckin' yuppie ass motherfuckers. Why do they come here to pretend to listen to the New African classical music?

69

They'd be better off at home goofin' around with their VCRs.

The intensity Brother Yusef's playing frequently forced ''the yappers'' (his name for the compulsive conversationalists) into an intimidated silence.

The couple at table number three, tried to pretend that the large boned, fiercely bearded, coal dark-skinned man playing the upright bass was not glaring at them, and playing his solo at them.

They couldn't pretend for long. He used the vacant spaces in their chit chat, filling in with rapidly swelling thumps and plunks, mimicking their conversation and weaving serious elements around it. It was an display of musical satire, rivaling Chocktos Animal suite.

The viciousness of his attack and the lengthening shadow of his hatred caused Mel Terry, piano man, leader of the quartet, to stage—whisper, ''Lighten up, brother Yusef, lighten up, baby.''

He finally returned to the theme after he had ground the couple into his musical palette. Some members of the audience, hip to and approving of what had happened, applauded enthusiastically. The majority, yuppies themselves, identified with the couple and responded to his vigorous solo with tepid hand claps.

Yusef Malik didn't acknowledge the approving applause or the lack of approval, it was all one to him. Fuck'em.

The end of the last set, Saturday night, the Blue Onion.

''Ladies and gentlemen, thank you for making the set, we'll be here 'til July 30th, so tell all your friends and neighbors . . . hah!''

Yusef Malik frowned in Mel Terry's direction. Cut the Tom shit, man . . .

''And now, the members of our quartet—first, on flute, tenor sax and alto, we have Mr. Hubert Frame.''

The applause rang out for the congenial Mr. Frame.

"On congas, bongoes, chekere, pandiero, agogo and a hundred other percussion instruments, Mr. Babalade Ofayemi."

Once again the applause meter was pushed upward.

"And next to last, the formidable, Mr. Yusef Malik."

The lightweight applause covered up Yusef Malik's growl from the corner of his mouth.

"Mel, I told you before, don't introduce me as Mr., I'm brother Yusef. Brother Yusef..."

Mel Terry ignored Yusef Malik's complaint with a smile.

"And last but not least, yours truly, Mel Terry, see ya next time, folks."

Yusef Malik toweled his bass strings off, propped the instrument in place and left the bandstand, trailed by the other members of the group, who paused to exchange pleasantries with the customers leaving the Blue Onion.

He sprawled out on one of the deck chairs in their dressing room, feeling drained from the pressures of doing three sets in front of largely unhip audiences, the people who used to come for the music and knew what they were receiving when the goods were delivered.

He stared up at the ceiling, wool gathering back to his days with Lord Ra, Sonny Be', Coltrane II, Cherry, Mondo, Miles (for a minute), Kirby Lester, the Chicago Quintet, the Avant Garde Group in Amsterdam.

"Yusef, how ya doin, man?"

He turned his attention from his memories to the pleasant Italian face of the Blue Onion owner, Max Pregasetti.

O.K., lets hear the latest bullshit.

"You got it, Max, you got it..."

"You meditatin' or something?"

"Naw, c'mon in, lets kick it."

Max Pregasetti bounced in, a real meatball of a man who attempted to look as though he cared about being dressed

71

in the latest fashions, but always failed.

Meat sauce splattered his shirt front, his trousers caught under the heels of his expensive Australian loafers and the gold chains around his neck were obscured by the rolls of sweaty fat.

Despite his unlikely appearance, Yusef dug him for two great traits; he was a jazz lover from the old school and he paid the band members promptly.

He folded his hands in front of his belly like a choir boy and stood beaming in front of Yusef Malik.

"Brother Malik, you was hot tonight, baby, I mean hot."

Yusef nodded slightly, almost a seated bow. Compliment from a jazz lover, an authentic devotee, was to be acknowledged.

Pregasetti bounced slightly from one foot to the other, a nervous habit that usually preceded something he felt ill at ease about saying.

The other members trickled in, feeling jovial. Mel Terry fingered a match book with the palomino haired woman's phone number on it in his front pocket.

You could get a lot of pussy in the Blue Onion, if you were willing to be just the least bit "nice."

Hubert Frame popped another dexie and flushed it down with half a bottle of Guiness Stout. Babalade Ofayemi drummed nervously on the edge of his dressing table.

It was frustrating to play for limited periods of time.

He never felt that he was really getting off until he had latched onto a six—eight rhythm for an hour or more.

Max greeted each individual, an expertly executed soul shake here, a soft slap on the back, a look of awe and respect.

"Max!" Yusef called to the club owner above the developing party atmosphere. A trio of groupies, two female and one male, had infiltrated the dressing room. It wouldn't be long before a few more made their way backstage.

Pregasetti cocked his head in Yusef's direction, "Yeah, Yusef?"

"What is it you were goin' to say before the brothers came in?"

The owner shuffled across the room and stood bouncing from foot to foot. He jammed his hammy fists into his sports coat pocket.

"Oh, nuttin' really, you know..."

Yusef cocked a malevolent—question mark eyebrow at him.

"C 'mon, man spit it out. You know it ain't like you to clam up."

Pregasetti stared at his shoes and then at a distant point before speaking.

"Uhh, well, actually, what I wanted to say—no big thing you know—but what I wanted to suggest, you know, is that maybe, you know, maybe you could go just a little easier on the clientele, you know what I mean? Now didn't get me wrong, Yusef. I'm on your side, you know that, but the customers..."

Babalade Ofayemi stopped playing nervous figures on the edge of the dressing room table. Yusef Malik's rages were really awesome to witness. The drummer settled back and watched Yusef gather himself up from his seat like a storm cloud.

He stood, a large boned 5'10", but when he raged he seemed twice as large. He towered over everyone in the room.

His voice was the lowest bass note he had ever played, and loud.

"Are you tryin' to tell me how to play my music?!"

Pregasetti's face turned purple and he shifted his head from side to side, a subconscious imitation of Stevie Wonder.

Bouncing lightly from left foot to right foot, his head

wobbling, he almost seemed to be dancing in place.

"Ahh, uhh, no Yusef, nuttin like that, I was just, you know...hah...going to suggest that, well, maybe, you could...uhh...you know, be a little more pleasant?!

Pregasetti's voice squeaked on the last three words. Yusef Malik stuffed his bristling beard into the owner's face and began to rumble out his words.

"Now you listen to me good, Max, 'cause I ain't gonna never say this again. For all I care your fuckin' customers can eat my shit, if you can find any of them worthy of the honor.

"Do you know who I am?!"

Bold streaks of sweat slid down the side of the owner's face as he nodded yes, yes, yes.

"I am Yusef Malik. I play the most imaginative bass since Mingus. I have played with Lord Ra, I have played with Sonny Be, with Kirby Lester, the Chicago Quintet, the Avant Garde Group and a collection of geniuses that most of your tin eared baboon customers have never heard of."

Max Pregasetti made a hopeless gesture with both hands at his side, to acknowledge Yusef Malik's greatness.

Malik wasn't shouting but his words boomed thru the stricken room.

"Don't you ever dare to tell me to be nice to these musical idiots who wander into this fuckin club. Do you hear me, Max Pregasetti!?"

"I hear you, Yusef, I hear you."

"Where in the fuck are you comin' from anyway?! I thought you had better sense than to talk to a man of my stature like that."

"Sorry, Yusef, sorry I pissed you off."

Malik turned suddenly from ragging Pregasetti's ass to push his beard into Mel Terry's face. The beard seemed to be ripple like snakes.

"And you my brother, cut this Minstrel show shit out."

Mel Terry drew his chin in and flicked his eyes from side to side, obviously afraid of the egomaniac confronting him.

"And one more thing, if you introduce me one more time as Mister, instead of Brother, I'm going to break your motherfuckin' fingers, one by one. O.K.?!"

Mel Terry jammed his hands into his pockets defensively. Brother Yusef Malik was known to have a terrible temper. He was like a grizzly bear when he got mad.

One evening Hubert Frame, wired up on a couple lines of pharmaceutical quality cocaine, found himself dodging Yusef's bass bow because he had broken in on his solo a chorus too soon.

The rage sputtered like a volcano as Malik pulled a fresh white linen three-quarter length shirt over his head, and adjusted a white cap over his semi-dreaded locks.

"What time is rehearsal tomorrow, Mel?"

The sudden change of rhythm and timbre caught them by surprise.

"Ohh, we figured, I figured we could chill out tomorrow, it's Sunday, you know?"

Mel Terry clenched the match book in his fist, Yusef Malik looked him up and down a few beats, his eyes reddening with pent-up fury.

"You mean to tell me, as raggedy as we been playin', we gon' take a fuckin' day off?! What the fuck are you talkin' about?! When we got into "Chano's Chant" this evening I thought all of us was droppin' our drawers 'n you talkin 'bout takin' a day off?!"

Mel Terry took a deep breath and sighed. The man, the brother was impossible to relate to socially, but he was the greatest bassist he'd ever played with.

People spoke of Oscar Pettirord, Jimmy Blanton, Mingus Reggie Workman, Jimmy Garrison, Paul Chambers and

Yusef Malik as though they were gods of the bass.

Yusef Malik knew he was a god, and never allowed them to forget it.

"Awright everybody, rehearsal tomorrow at two p.m., Yusef is right we got to get it tighter."

Malik stood in the open door and smiled viciously at each person in the room before going out and closing the door softly,

Max Pregasetti pulled a soiled white cotton handkerchief from his back pocked and swabbed his brow with it.

He hated to be clubbed in the head like that, in front of other people, but he felt it was worth it. After all, wasn't Yusef Malik the greatest bass player in the world.

Sometimes it paid to take a little crap, if you were lookin out for the future, The future for Max Pregasetti was producing and writing music for the Mel Terry Quartet, featuring Yusef Malik.

He swabbed his neck. The records we'll sell will go down in history and make us piles of dough.

"O.K., guys, gather round, I got bread to pass out. Where did Yusef go? I didn't pay him yet."

"It don't matter where he went, just be sure you got his money when he see you again,"

Babalade announced in his sing song Nigerian accent.

Max Pregasetti nodded in agreement and pulled a fat wallet from his breast pocket.

Riga gritted her teeth together, Professor Bronte folded his arms across his chest and lowered his chin to his collar bone, a rare gesture of exasperation for him.

He signalled for her to stop in mid-passage. She was attempting to play the opining movement of a modern piece of music by Lade Sat, called "Sun Food."

Riga lowered her violin, waiting for Professor Bronte's

critique.

She loved the modern works for violin, they were so challenging and complicated to play. And frustrating.

"Riga, how can I say this?"

She waited patiently for the Professor to speak. He was such a dear, patient man, willing to spend all the time necessary for her to grasp a point.

He unfolded and refolded his arms twice, a study in frustration. Finally he stood in front of her, a chubby caricature of Toscanini.

"Your technique is wonderful for this piece, absolutely wonderful, you understand?"

She nodded numbly. "What is the problem if my technique is right?"

"The problem is that you're not bringing the kind of soulfulness to this work that it needs. You understand? The problem is soul."

Once again she nodded. Wasn't the soul of the work built into the technique? Professor Bronte seemed to read her mind.

"Riga, please believe me, the soul of a work is not automatically revealed because you are playing well, you must bring another dimension to the work. Now, let's try again..."

She adjusted the handkerchief, placed the violin properly between chin and shoulder and began to play the syncopated melodies of Lade Sat's "Sun Food."

Professor Bronte paced up and down half way across the studio as she played. Suddenly he stopped pacing and moved quickly in her direction.

"Riga, this needs to be played like American Negro music, like jazz! You understand?"

She stared at him blankly. American Negro music? Jazz? In all of the fifteen years she had been a student of the

77

violin she had never attempted to play jazz. In Lithuania jazz meant Louis Armstrong, Bessie Smith perhaps, or maybe a little Dizzy Gillespie.

Some of the wild ones had preciously guarded tapes of John Coltrane, Miles Davis, Wynton Marsalis, Oscar Peterson and others, but for the conservatory trained musicians, music was European classical period.

Professor Bronte's eyes lit up.

"Of course you do not understand, you are not familiar with this music. You must see it, hear it, absorb it to understand it."

She propped her violin on her left thigh and nodded again. Professor Bronte plunged his thumbs into his vest pockets and puffed his chest out.

"I myself, will expose you to this music and then you will understand how 'Sun Food' should be played."

Yusef Malik kept a steady pace for his six mile run, twice around the big field in Washington Park, not too fast, not too slow.

The run accomplished, he walked quickly to his compact Japanese car, focusing on the next steps of his daily routine.

Home (an uncluttered apartment on Kimbark Avenue, in Hyde Park), shower, answer phone calls, juice and fruit brunch, listen to the new tape of Bismillah Khan, make the two p.m. rehearsal at the Blue Onion.

He drove expertly thru the streets of his hometown, cataloging new scenes, buildings, faces.

Yusef was proud of his sense of discipline, the dedication he brought to his art.

"None of that dope—junky—shit for me, if music ain't enough to get me high then I'll never be high."

Music was his life and the music he called "The New African Classical Music" was his blood bank.

"Someday these fools will look up and discover what we really have up in here."

He played a tape of Ravel's Quartet in F Major as he showered, humming along with the sections he liked. Music, music, music, all is music.

Drying himself after the shower, he studied his body in the full length mirror. Hmmmmmmm...not bad for a forty-two-year-old-brother who used to suck on the night and never put a cork in the liquor bottle.

Have to do a few more push ups...

Phone calls: "Yusef, this is Doris, call me when you get a chance."

Wonder what she wants?

Yusef couldn't figure it out, the more assertive he was, the more arrogant, the more opinionated he was, the more he was liked by a certain kind of woman. Doris Rawls was a good example; an entrepreneur, well read, been everywhere, full of herself.

"You know something, Doris there's just one thing wrong with you, you think you know every fuckin' thing."

He had, by design, a completely different kind of relationship with four African-American women.

Doris Rawls could stand toe to toe with him in any argument that concerned geopolitics, art, history, finance, public relations, psychology, racial relations and a number of other subjects that might spring up.

He had discovered after a few stabs at it, they were better off being friends than lovers. Doris Rawls wasn't completely convinced of his conclusion.

"I think we'd really have a nice thing going, brother Malik, if you let your guard down a little."

Sandra Waters, a show business attorney, was always available to offer advice or to go jogging with. He wasn't quite certain whether it would be to their advantage to become lovers.

Why spoil a good business relationship for the sake of an orgasm?

He jokingly referred to Linda Price and Francine Du Valier as his "harem." The ladies knew each other in a peripheral, hip way, and that they were both lovers of Yusef Malik.

He/they were honest with each other and during the course of their two-year involvement had only experienced one miscue.

Yusef apologized to both of them for having made the faux pas and stood in a distant corner for a month, to determine which way the wind would blow or the fur would fly.

Francine pulled him out of the corner and turned him around with an hour of frank talk.

"Yusef, look, let's get something straight, O.K.? I know I'm not the only woman in the world who digs you, O.K.?

"Now don't get me wrong, I'm not seriously into sharing anything. I'm the kind of woman who feels that everything I have is mine.

"I feel you're mine, O.K.? but I know that it would be foolish for me to come onto you like that, O.K.?

"So, let's work this out like African adults, O.K."

They worked it out.

They spent alternate weekends with him whenever he wanted their company and, in the interim, got about the business of what they felt they had to do in Life.

The situation was not a hang up for either of them. Some of the people who knew about their arrangement thought it was "unusual," others felt that it was a hip—modern thing.

Babalade Ofayemi often complimented Yusef on his success.

"You're doing something a lot of brothers at home can't do well."

The women were completely different types, which seemed

to help matters. Linda was heavily into the spiritual side of things. She loved to go to the park to listen to the rustling of the trees, or to the lake to listen to the water lap against the rocks.

Francine was earthier, sexier, but they both shared an Africentric perspective. They wore African designed clothes, ate African foods, worshipped in the West African tradition and ignored as much of America's Eurocentrism as possible.

"I can't be bothered by all that sick shit." Yusef was the first to acknowledge that his relationship with the two women "freed" him up to create more, to explore sections of himself that he had previously neglected.

"You'd be amazed how much creative energy is lost, runnin' around out there trying to find a clean piece o' pussy."

The sisters were both in their late 30s, successful in their fields (Linda Price, the spiritualist, college level sociology instructor. Francine DuValier, export-import. He often wondered how many of Linda's kente cloth outfits had come thru Francine's hands) and weren't programmed for the idea of a conventional marriage.

Francine: "I went the route for ten yrs, from 20 to 30, had the child, the lawn with the husband attached to the lawn mower, the bills, the whole avocado and I was unhappy.

"I don't know, maybe I'll think differently in the future but, for right now, I have exactly what I want—the attention of an attractive, creative, inspiring man who plays with my ears just the way I like to have them played with. And plays with my head with his music. I'm happy."

Linda: "Who was it that said, 'A cynic knows the price of everything and the value of nothing?' I'm not a cynic.

"I take a lot of pride in thinking and feeling that I'm into values and not prices.

"Yusef would be a superb value on any market and I feel

privileged to share a part of my life with him.

"He's an extremely fragile, sensitive human being who makes me feel important, needed. Beneath that warrior's facade is the soul of a beautiful child."

Yusef Malik sliced bananas, cantaloupe, apples, half an orange and a kiwi into his cereal bowl, doused a few tablespoons of yogurt on the mixture and sprinkled wheat germ over everything.

He sprawled in his breakfast nook, listening to Master Bismillah Khan blow the shenai, leisurely spooning his fruit up, absorbing the shimmering sound of the huge cottonwood tree in front of his kitchen window.

Damn! I really hate that I never got a chance to play with Bird.

The thought was like a recurring thread of frustration.

Yeahhh, I've played with the best we have right now but Bird was the best for all time, like me.

The gush of egotism straightened his shoulders, sucked his gut in. Who knows? Maybe I will have a chance to play with Bird someday.

He finished off his fruit brunch with a flourish and began preparation to make the two o'clock rehearsal.

Can't be late, not good for the New African classical musician's image.

It would've been impossible not to notice them sitting at table three, fifteen minutes before the beginning of the set, the chubby white haired guy who looked like a symphony orchestra conductor and the beautiful young woman with the intense grey eyes.

Hubert Frame whispered to Mel Terry as they mounted the stage.

"Now that is what I call a beautiful white woman."

Yusef studied the couple and the people surrounding them,

something a stage performer was privileged to do as he faced the audience.

They weren't father and daughter, that seemed fairly obvious. And he was obviously not the sugar daddy type, not with a glass of Seven-Up and a draft beer gracing their barren table.

"Uh one, uh two, uh one two three!"

The Sunday rehearsal was validated by the first piece, a boppish thing written by Max Pregasetti. They were tight, right in the groove, crisp.

The audience was with them. Yusef tried not to betray his surprise. Well, I'll be damned. Maybe there is hope for these burned out yuppie assholes.

His attention returned to the old man and the young woman. He was doing a bit of animated whispering in her ear. She looked slightly puzzled but nodded as though she were in agreement.

Very interesting. Very...

The piece came to an end as though every nerve ending of the music had been frozen into compact cube. The audience exploded with appreciative applause.

Yusef Malik took inventory of the men on stage with him; Mel, Hubert and Babalade. They had the kind of cohesion happening that comes from playing together for a while, rehearsing strenuously, being sensitive to each other.

They were all writers, supplying the quartet with a wonderful collection of pieces.

"Mambo Mandela" was Hubert Frame's contribution. He signalled for Babalade to lay the foundation for a slow, lushly accented mambo, slipped Yusef in, gave the piano an opportunity to doodle throughout and leaped on top of all of it with flute playing that reminded Yusef of Bismillan Khan's shenai.

Pausing for more applause they followed "Mambo Mandela" with Babalade Ofayemi's "Ibeji."

"I wrote this piece for my twin sisters back home, Taiwo, the one who comes first and Kehinde, the one who comes after."

"Ibeji" was two different moods in the same groove.

Babalade tried to make them understand while they were rehearsing the piece; "I want you to give me the feeling of two different people who went thru the same birth channel."

Ofayemi's mouth was split by a smile at the conclusion of their musical reading.

"That's what I mean, like that, that's what I want," he called out to the quartet above the sounds of the applause.

The evening was going well. Yusef nodded politely in response to the applause. So far, so good. No "white drunks," no yuppie couples sweating and climbing all over each other because the music had stirred their libidos, no Black people overreacting to the music because they felt the need to assert their connection to the music.

He locked eyes with the young white woman at table three. She seemed to be in a hypnotic state, her eyes glazed her mouth relaxed and smiling. The old man had stuck his thumbs into his vest pockets and leaned back with an air of satisfaction on his face, midway into his second draft beer.

"Berimbau Bass" was Yusef Malik's contribution to the evening's first set. He was fascinated by the African-Brazilian berimbau, a bow shaped instrument with a gourd resonator, that was used as a "time keeper" for the playing of the African—Brazilian martial art called Capoeira Regional and the older, more ritualized style called Capoeira Angola.

He had transcribed a rhythm called "Angola" from the berimbau gunga to the bass. Mel Terry thought it was a masterpiece.

"I ain't never heard no shit like it. The rhythm is totally

insistent, but at the same time it has nuances on top of nuances.''

Yusef played the simple figures that made "Angola," added Babalade playing counter point on pandiero, used Mel's percussion piano as a backdrop and gave the singing voice to Hubert's alto saxophone.

Several Brazilians visiting the club had gushed over him about the piece.

"Tuda bem, senhor, tuda bem."

The fugal complexity of "Angola" grabbed Yusef's total focus for a few choruses, forcing him to close his eyes for a moment.

When he re-opened his eyes it seemed that the woman's face at table three had become luminous. He studied her expression; it wasn't groupie—goofy, it was something else.

They played into his solo on "Berimbau Bass," it was time to stretch his imagination to the sky. In the vacuum left by the other instruments, Yusef re-established the theme of "Angola" three times, and then played the notes backwards.

He took note of the expression on her face, it was flexible, absorbent. The old man prodded her with his elbow, as though to emphasize a point, and excused himself.

Yusef smiled at his departure. That draft beer has hit the old dude's bladder.

The old man's departure left the two of them alone. Riga leaned forwarded intently. So, this is the jazz music.

She studied the attitudes and postures of the men on stage; Mel Terry, the pianist tinkled in a few notes from time to time. She was puzzled about the entrances and exits he took.

The music gave the appearance of being thrown together, but she knew that this appearance was a deception. It was obvious that whatever they were doing would collapse if there was one miscue.

She tried to pat her foot to the rhythms that Yusef was

weaving in and out of in his solo, and gave up the effort.

The music was complex. She counted times and discovered a four/four time that led into a two/four time that segued into a six/eight and then back into a four/four.

Yusef plumbed the elements of "Angola." She felt him going deeper and resisted for a few beats.

I can't understand this.

Her resistance was skillfully pushed aside by the brutal insistence of his ideas.

Come with me come with me come with me...

Professor Bronte slid back into the seat beside her, studied the expression on her face for a moment and leaned back feeling satisfied with his experiment.

He didn't like African-American music in general, but he respected the complex nature of it, and he felt certain that Riga had absorbed enough of the flavor to be able to infuse Lade Sat's "Sun Food" with the proper spirit.

Yusef Malik used space and time in a way that delighted Riga; she felt good about the music, stimulated and slightly bewildered.

Yusef literally danced the music to a conclusion by performing a little ginga with the bass. The people around her erupted into applause, shouts of pleasure—"Yeahhh!"

Riga was too stunned to applaud at the end of the set. The lights came up, people milled around them, it was over.

Professor Bronte stood and asked, "Well, what do you think? You think you understand better what I've been saying?

"Yes, yes, I think so," she answered in a faraway voice. Yusef Malik spoke to her from the stage with a questioning, eyebrow. "Well, what do you think of that?"

She walked to the edge of the stage apron and reached out to shake his hand. They exchanged a firm handshake, the Professor beaming over her shoulder.

"Thank you," she said, and backed away, melting into the crowd filing out.

Yusef strolled near the water line on the beach at 57th Street, something he often did after the last set at the club.

He felt too keyed up to go home, didn't want to hang out with the band members (or the groupies) and felt no urge to call Francine or Linda.

He stared at the shimmering image of the moon on the lake and thought of the idea for a piece of music.

I'll call it "Black Moon"

The moonlight on the water, the glistening of the downtown lights, the billions of stars overhead, the distant sound of city noises made him feel as though he were a creature from another place.

He walked a few yards away from the gently lapping waves and sprawled on the sand, cradling his head in his hands to stare at the sky.

God, how stars are the most beautiful things in the world and people run around buying diamonds and stuff to put on their bodies; what they need to do is put some stars in their eyes.

He closed his eyes to feel the clusters of stars bursting behind his eyelids.

I wonder who that woman was? If we could only get more people to listen to the New African Classical Music with that kind of intensity. And the old bird with her, wonder who he was?

Musical themes were triggered in his subconsciousness by the lapping of the water against the shore, a stray car horn honking, ethereal voices whispering in both of his ears simultaneously rhythms.

He sat up slowly, he could sense the cool air of dawn coming over the horizon, followed by gorgeous streaks of dull, blue and yellow.

87

How many dawns have I seen, in how many places?

The southeastern coast of Spain, Tokyo, Paris, Amsterdam, Quebec, Berlin, Geneva, Madrid, Lakeside, Michigan.

He stood, placed his fists on his hips and scowled at the lights that were being extinguished downtown.

It's always the same, lovely at night, fucked up in the day time. O well . . .

He jammed his hands into his pockets and walked away from the beach, time for practice.

Riga felt the last notes of "Sun Food" throbbing away from her violin, each note an invitation to beauty, clarity, love, rhythm, sensuality.

She slowly removed the violin from beneath her chin and dabbed at the perspiration on her top lip. She had "felt" her way thru Lade Sat's "Sun Food," playing some of the parts in a way that made it seem as though she were improvising.

She had allowed the music to dominate her, using her techniques as a release valve.

Professor Bronte leaned over to pat her on the cheek, his eyes glistening.

"Yes, now you understand, Riga. You truly understand."

Riga smiled. "Yes, I do understand, I must find out more about this music called New African Classical and the people responsible for creating it."

Mo' Music

It was clearly a freedom buy for all parties, plus maximum benefits. David and Martha had put their coins together for tickets to Ghana, West Africa, and I was chosen to be the caretaker of their luxurious 8th floor apartment in South Commons, overlooking Lake Michigan.

No idea how it came about; one minute I was in deepest Los Angeles, battling Crips, Bloods, the freeways and Hollywood producers, next minute I'm in Chicago, sipping birthday cake and agreeing to water the family's hallucigenic plants during their absence.

For three weeks, I was going to be responsible for the plants, have the honor of representing the household in the local bodega and get my full share of staring at the lovely little boats down in the lake.

It was the perfect set up for a honeymoon. I called this outrageously gorgeous Choctaw-Ukranian woman in California to come visit me...

"Yes, I'll be there on Friday."

"But today is Sunday, what're you planning to do, hitch hike?"

"No, silly, I can't fly, I'm afraid..."

This, from a person who strolled around nude on the parapets of four story buildings.

"O.K., lover, see you on Friday."

"I'll be on an early train, call you when I get in."

"You better."

Nothing to do 'til Friday but stare into Lake Michigan. I have never lived higher than two stories above the ground in Chicago and now, come Friday, there we were, doing one on one orgies miles above the ground.

"I'll only be able to stay five days."

"Let's do the best we can with that."

We fell out of the sky a few times, started up rhythms that sloshed water out of the lake basin, brutalized each other with tenderness...

"Did you...?

"I did, five times, did you?"

"Yes, I'm still doing it..."

We filled up on Billie "You're My Thrill" Holiday, Billie "Why This Strange Desire," Billie, this desire that keeps mounting higher, Billie, Billie, Billie...

We opened the lake front's light show at night and closed it for dawn streaked nature shows. We entertained no guests.

We couldn't predict the ending of this dreamtime and when the numbers came up, we simply placed our cards on the table, face up.

"I'm so glad you came."

"Is that a pun?"

It took a whole night of fussy sleeping for me to get used to the idea of a bed without Semenchuk.

She had been my sweet thang for five days and nights and now she was gone.

I mentally kicked myself in the ass for days after she detrained, feeling stupid. I hadn't told her that I loved her. I hadn't made love with her as often as she wanted to make love...

"But, baby, it's 3 a.m., we've already made love three times already."

My aptitude for self-condemnation was exhausted a half-day later, I've never been one to live too seriously in the past. Time is too precious for that.

I was an ambulating bachelor with a freak pad, money in pocket and time on my hands. I started making sorties down to the restaurant-bar for slow lunches and gin 'n tonics.

I knew it would only take a few days for some beautiful sister to discover me, I could daydream about my honeymoon woman in my spare time, later.

South Commons "Common Ground," was where the Black upwardly mobile folks tripped for their rendezvous and adulterous coup d'etats. Nice place.

It took two whole days of veal scallopini with mushrooms and wild rice, ushered by a dry white wine that rang bells on my palate before we managed to fall into each others orbits.

"If you're married, seriously connected or expecting someone, please ignore this invitation to have dinner with me."

Gorgeous, cocoa-beige colored sister with Ashanti earrings and ebony dimples in her checks. She must've read the note four or five times before asking the waitress-messenger, "Which one is he?"

I had zoomed in on her the minute she mounted the bar stool and the bartender whisked over with a glass of white wine. I have no idea what I would've done if she had told the waitress, "Tell him to get lost."

Cocoa colored ensemble, full up front and not too ample behind, sweet buttered thighs, regal bearing.

"How did you know I hadn't had dinner?"

"My sensitive vibes told me, shall we start with dessert and go backward?"

We wandered into holding hands after the salad, and was doing some serious knee to knee knocking by the time the steamed red snapper was placed in front of us.

She called herself a "fun woman" who believed in the power of positive reaction and took herself seriously.

"Who says you're free if you behave like someone in jail?"

We discovered that we were neighbors...

"I live on the 14th floor."

She was an executive in the Urban League and had a healthy appetite... "Hmmmmmmmmm that was absolutely delicious, thank you."

She signalled for the second bottle of wine; "This one is on me, do you mind?"

It was, I felt, a moment stolen from a rare painting. We sipped our wine and explored each other's minds and attitudes.

"Please tell me your name. The man has paid for my dinner and I don't even know his name."

I told her what my name was and asked for hers.

"Rose Bahia LeVeau."

I sucked in a deep breath when she said it, never will forget it; "Rose Bahia LeVeau," originally from New Orleans, Louisiana.

She had a musical voice and loved laughing. I was enchanted by the lady. After dinner, the excess wine, a Venetian dessert, a superior cognac and wonderful espresso, we strolled around inside the South Commons Complex, enjoying each other's company.

"What now?"

"Well, in the movies and in certain yuppie bars on the Near Northside, I would say—'Your place or mine?'"

She frowned for the first time that afternoon. I quickly cleaned up.

"Fortunately, we are not movie stars and we are not yuppies in the bars on the Near Northside."

She flashed a smile at me and gave my hand a reassuring

squeeze, we were going to play for the real stuff, nothing flaky, nothing dizzy, nothing simple, we were going to explore complexities.

I was tempted to ask her if she wanted to be examined for AIDS and all other nastiness the following day, but I checked myself.

I had already made a slight boo boo, no need to compound things. But I was anxious to let her know that my sexual history included condoms until it came down to a seriously worded agreement.

She was obviously in tune with that, I could tell from the way she kissed. We took the elevator up to her place, we laughed at silly jokes, she rode back down to the eighth floor with me, I rode back up to her floor.

We didn't want to call the evening to an end. "Rose I can't remember when I've had so much fun. Such a good time with someone I've just met. You know what I mean?"

"Yes, I do know."

"Usually I'm the kind of guy who wants to turn his face to the wall because the pressure of getting to know some one..."

"I understand."

The final kiss was understated, almost sedate

"Hate to say goodnight, but I'm a working girl."

We made a til-death-do-us-part date for the following day, to continue our exploration.

"What time?"

"Same time."

"I may be a few minutes late, I'm going to change into something green before we meet."

"What's green supposed to do?"

"Green is for hope, promise, goodies..."

He sat in the modified black barber's chair that David had

93

inherited from his history, mind spooling out fragrant memories of his recent honeymoon with Semenchuk, the Choctaw-Ukranian sister.

He loved her because of the peculiar schizoidness that meshed in a way he had never thought about.

The Choctaw gene gave her an aboriginal feeling for naturalness. He clearly imaged them stopping the car beyond Malibu, leaping out with two blankets, one to go under and one to cover.

Sometimes they didn't have a blanket at all. And there was her love of bread, salt, vodka and dancing, Ukraine.

She gave him a lot to think about, the lake gave him a lot to think about, the miniaturized people scurrying around in the streets, being eight floors above the ground gave him a lot to think about.

He spread the futon in front of the crystal ball picture window, poured a double Remy Martin, clicked off the lights and voyeured from one apartment window to another.

They had become familiar strangers; the nymphomaniac directly across the concourse, holding her heels in the air as though she were giving birth to the shuddering man laboring between her thighs.

The dancer on tippy toes, the closet transvestite, the bulimic, assembling a tray of food to feed on while she stared at the television. The odd couple, the after work party folk, the telescope addicts, the men and women who tripped thru their apartments naked, the desperate people sitting next to their telephones.

He took a long sip of cognac and sprawled out to stare up at the stars. Rose Bahia LeVeau.

Know how it is when you want something to happen sooner than its going to happen? It was wearing on me like that.

I jogged myself silly on the track in the morning, showered

and went back to bed. It was going to be a long day, I had to be patient.

I woke up an hour later and read the newspaper . . . the Bush Administration was trying to push us back into chattel slavery. The talk shows on television were more pathetic and gruesome than usual; "My dad had kids by all his daughters. Yeah, I kinda think Mom knew, yeah, I think so."

What time are we getting together? 4:30-5:00? Twelve noon? I sat in the barber's chair trying to read a book. Who in the hell could concentrate on the simple stuff in a book when the lake was right below you?

Gorgeous Chicago stuffed full of people who would never be found in any other city on Earth. Where else could you find real Bohemians? Polish sausages from Maxwell and Halsted (enough cholesterol to blind you), Soul food in Glady's Restaurant, southern friendliness in a northern city (counterpointed by Uzi bullets splattering around, if you happened to be on the wrong corner).

The negative meant nothing to me. I didn't want to pay any attention to the Mafia foundation, the insidiousness of the Irish political shenanigans, Jewish money manipulation, African-American consumership levels, Asian bullshit, none of that. I was focused on the absolute positive, Rose Bahia LeVeau.

Funny how a woman can affect a man. He can be as stable and stiff as a brick 'til the right woman comes along.

What happens? How do they do it?

I spent an hour (from 1 p.m.–2 p.m.) pondering that one. I knew what a woman was/is. I've had friends, lovers, enemies, people who were women and I could never figure out what it was that made them women, that essence of something that is more than thighs, breasts and buttocks.

I seriously considered going back down to the track for another workout, changed my mind and did sit-ups instead.

The one thing I knew I didn't want to do was start sipping on anything. If I got high, I wanted it to be with Rose Bahia LeVeau and we'd start from scratch.

Three-thirty p.m., I settled into a tub full of Skin So Soft...I was goin to be smellin' good, lookin' good and feelin' good when we met.

The intended long bath was cut short by a phone. Rose? Had I given her my number? I splashed out of the tub and ran naked thru the front room. If one of the voyeurs was at work they'd have something to see.

"Hello?"

"Hi, may I speak to Marvin, please?"

"What number are you calling?"

"294-7582."

"You've dialed the wrong number."

"This isn't 294-7582?"

"Never was."

"What number is this?"

"None of your business!"

I slammed the phone into the cradle and stood there dripping and fuming. Always some shit waiting for you on the line I could smell the game coming up, somebody was calling to sell something or, in some way, trying to take advantage of the person answering the phone.

What the hell, the rhythm of my bath was broken now, nothing to do but dress and get onto the scene a little early. I decided to go casual-California on her, aloha pau shirt, slacks, Spanish net loafers.

I trimmed a few stray grey hairs from my mustache and beard, dashed a finger of Monsieur Houbigant on both cheeks and strutted out. I was ready.

My plan was to go down to the Common Ground place an order for two Poulet Basque dinners and sit at the bar hunched over a glass of cognac, looking suave 'til the lady put in her appearance. I didn't mind being early for Rose Bahia LeVeau.

I hit the ground floor at 3:51 p.m. and started my cake walk to the cafe. I caught sight of the last three as they turned the corner.

Was the brother carrying a Gon Bop on his head? I hurried around the corner to check out the procession,

Yeahhh, he was carrying a drum and four other brothers in the procession were also carrying axes. One ol' ugly lookin' junjun but the congas were fiber glass and sleek.

I have to call it a procession because that's what the twelve of them resembled. They were dressed in various stages of African attire, Reeboks with caftans, stuff like that.

I pulled up on the rear guard.

"Uhhh, where you brothers going with the drums?"

The young blood stared at me (none of them seemed older than twenty) like I had insulted him. I knew it was just a way of responding to a stranger and didn't trip on it.

The man strolling beside him answered, "We goin' over here to git down."

Damn! What would be a better way to kill an hour than with a posse of cold blooded congueros?

"Mind if I tag along?"

The young blood that I had originally questioned relayed my request to the leader.

"Hey Skull! He wanna know if he can git with this?"

Skull grunted, "Ain't no thang."

The telepathy operating had probably given Skull my name, age, time of arrival and possible proficiency on congas. I knew I could play them. Shit, I had jammed with Armando Peraza and Mongo Santamaria a few times, and had twenty years of practice behind me. I put out vibes for the quinto.

We were parading past "Common Ground" before I fully

97

realized what, "We goin over here to git down..." really meant. We were going across State Street and into the projects.

It felt weird to be a part if this gang walking past the early cocktail types. I caught glances of pity, superiority, and class consciousness.

We could have been a collection of homeless orphans, nasty ass criminals, ugly ducklings. My ambivalence was operating at a feverish level.

I wanted to be inside the "Common Ground," sipping my cognac and looking suave. But on the other hand I was with my people, we were going to play the drums. By this time the gang had somehow slowed down to suck me into the center of the procession.

"Where you from, man ?" Somebody asked me out of the corner of his mouth. My shoes, well tailored jeans and Kona gold shirt had already been properly noted and catalogued.

"I'm from here." I answered truthfully as we straggled into the ugly quadrangle that separated one civilian penitentiary sandwich box from the next one.

We had never been forced to live in the projects, while I was growing up in Chicago. Blessed Lord, Thank Heaven.

We lived in basements, in coal storage bins, in kleenex boxes turned upside down, but not the projects. Again Thank You Lord in Heaven above...made a quick, surreptitious time check—4:08 p.m. I had just about an hour top give whatever we were going to get into.

Skull loomed in my face, a grimace on his face that I think he meant to be a smile.

"You good?"

"I know how to play."

"You wanna smoke some herb 'fore we git down?"

I had to strain to hear him from ten feet away, the noise

level inside the quadrangle was at a bedlam decibel.

"Yeah, why not?"

I didn't feel I was in a position to refuse to smoke anything. I was beginning to feel like a captive-guest. A weirdly uncomfortable, feeling. No one had acted overtly hostile toward me but the vibe wasn't cool. I was an outsider, inside.

The quadrangle was many studies of madness; men and women screamed at each other behind the wire mesh that screened the porches from the top floor to the first floor.

Drugs, drugs sales, drug use, all kind of drugs flowed back and forth in the quadrangle. Casual scenes of dumb-shit cruelty were everywhere; mothers beating children, children beating other children, teenagers battling each other.

And above it all, the bedlam decibel level, everyone playing whatever they wanted to play, and we were going to add to the mixture with drums and cowbells.

Skull motioned with his enormous head for me to follow him. It was pretty obvious why they called him Skull. Four of the gang fell in behind us.

Where were we going to get high? Why did we have to go any place? Everybody was doing everything right there. Skull read my mind.

"Were goin' up to my pad I got my stash up in my pad."

We suddenly plunged into an opening and started up the grimmest stairs I'd ever seen. The piss stains and stench, relieved here and there by random piles of turds, vomit, raw garbage and stuff I couldn't identify in the dim light littered the steps.

When the person behind me said, "Watch yo step, there's a section missin' here," I felt like a man on his way to be raped.

I didn't know where I was, I didn't know these people, they weren't my people, they were creatures from the projects, they knew their way up'n down stairwells like these.

I had seventy-five dollars in my pocket. Should I just simply offer it to them? What were they going to do with me? Should I fight back when we reached the brutal section on the eight floor? He unlocked two locks to let us in, motioned for me to enter. I didn't want to enter but I disguised the feeling.

Crazy looking place. The walls were painted in red, black and green zebra stripes; garish paintings littered the walls and it stank with the odor of thousands of hours of unfumigated marijuana smoking.

"Skull like that herb," the brother behind me whispered. The four young brothers settled onto a rag-bag sofa, a mattress on the floor, I was left the place of honor, a collapsing dinette chair.

A dim light glanced off the walls, it could have been midnight or midday. Skull disappeared for a moment and reappeared with a zip lock bag filled with greenish marijuana. He began to roll joints, glancing at me from time to time. I felt like raw meat. But there was another kind of feeling taking hold too. I was a survivor. I am a survivor. I had paid my dues. What the fuck was I feeling whimpy about?

Raw joints, no sweet wine to go with it, no munchies stuff, no Trane, Bird, Diz or Miles. We wouldn't have been able to hear nuances anyway.

I grabbed the undecided looks they exchanged and decided to play thru them. They were shrewd, cunning maybe, but I was convinced that they weren't smarter than me.

I jumped out on them after three hits on this awful herb. It tasted like dolls hair and Camel cigarettes. O my goodness! Are we smoking PCP?

"How long you been playin'?"

"Years, since I was a young blood, like y'all."

"Why you wanna play with us ?"

O Father, spare me another hit on this terrible shit, I'd

rather be drinking Old Grand Dad or something.

"Cause when I saw y'all walkin thru South Commons with your axes I said to myself these have got to be some of the baddest young motherfuckers on the planet and I wanna jam with 'em.

They released something like a collective burp, I moved on as quickly as a dying stand-up comic. I rushed thru the history of Chicago conga drumming (57th Street/The Point/63rd Street/ Beach/The Northside/Washington Park), I told nasty jokes, I detoured them away from the premeditated thing they had in mind and when I stood up and said, "Hey, lets git on with it! Skull was enthusiastic.

"Yeah!"

The treacherous part was negotiating our way back down that horrible staircase. I think, there were several times when I almost didn't make it.

Once, on the third floor, Skull suddenly remembered that he had left his last joint upstairs and wanted me and what's-his-name to go back up with him.

I pretended I hadn't heard and kept the motion in place. Fifteen minutes to five by my watch.

My heart felt like a drum by the time we emerged from the entrance. The brothers who had been left to mind the drums looked a bit surprised to see me.

They were passing a couple quarts of "Bang" beer around and a joint. Yeahhh, I had escaped a set up but I wasn't in the clear yet just because I was outside in the quadrangle.

I could see, to my left, three people being strangled, to my right a man was having his throat cut with a butter knife. A twelve-year-old girl was having sex with a middle aged man at 12 o'clock high. Was it rape?

It would've been impossible to imagine what was going on behind me. One of the brothers started up a question rhythm on a drum. I sat down behind the quinto to try to answer him.

I received a few curious looks but nobody said anything.

Skull lumbered up and asked, "You got the top?"

I immediately pushed the quinto out to him, "Not unless you want it?"

He struggled with the muscles in his face to give me a real smile, refused my offer and settled down beside me on the bench. Everybody moved over.

A junjun, four congas, two cowbells and a fucked up looking chekere. We were going to take the neighborhood back home.

A few natural music lovers circled us, dope, wine, beer, whiskey, gin bottles in hand. The junjun man struck a basic pattern, the bass conga (Skull) got with him and the other two drums laid in that solid foundation that causes people to dance.

We had a serious problem, they couldn't hold a rhythm. And the rhythm they were attempting to hold was so unimaginative I felt like screaming.

We made fits and starts. The cowbell and chekere players were project individualists, sheer improvisation from gong to shake. We accidentally stumbled onto a six-eight for five minutes and I tried to ride it with the quinto but no go.

Damn! They had these beautiful fiber glass Gon Bops but couldn't play a lick.

I suspected the drums had been stolen.

"Why don't you take the bottom for a while?"

Skull was giving me the bass, an exchange. I stood up as though I was going to change places with him and slowly burrowed into the circle around us. It was the closest thing to a disappearing act I had ever performed.

Skull, the leader, saw what I was doing immediately.

"Hey! hey! Where you going?"

The prey was escaping, the sacrifice had made it to the

edge of the circle, the escapee was dodging cars racing across State Street.

"Hey! Catch that dude!"

The free man, slightly winded, was opening the doors to the leather and pine scented atmosphere of the Common Ground.

"Good evening, sir, would you like to make a reservation for dinner?"

"Yes, a table for two at 5:30."

"Very good, sir. Smoking or non-smoking?"

"Non-smoking."

I staggered to the bar and climbed up on a seat. Thank goodness there were backs on the seats, I needed support. "Remy Martin, double, please."

I hunched over my drink trying to look suave, my heart tripping like timbales. At least it was keeping proper time.

Rose Bahia LeVeau made her entrance five minutes later a gorgeous dream in egg yolk yellow and mint green.

"Been waiting long?"

"Nawww, just got here a few minutes ago."

We traded a sweet peck on the lips before she occupied the seat next to me.

"Now then, I don't have to tell you what I've been doing, I've been on my j.o.b. all day. What've you been doing with yourself?"

I took a sip from my snifter and tried to sound as blase as possible.

"Oh, not a helluva lot, a little this a little that. You know how it is when you're killing time."

"Mr. Jones, a table for two?"

We strolled into the dining room arm in arm, my legs slightly rubbery, a smile on my face. Killing time? Yeahh, that's what I've been doing, killing time with Skull 'n the gang and they're still doing it, killing time.

103

Nostalgia

"Eschikagou," the Native Americans called it, the place where the wild onions stink. The banks of the Chicago River still stink, but the stench doesn't come from wild onions.

The lake gives off a ripe odor too, 'specially on tropical nights when the fish have bunched up for a little midnight fun. But these are abstract, almost impersonal memories, nothing like the sizzling thoughts provoked by the sniffing of fingers that once identified one teenaged girl from her sister, a carefully guarded perfume.

There are ghosts strolling East and West on 55th Street, North and South on King Drive, begging to be redeemed by people who cannot remember who they were. The ghosts, like the memories of past thunderstorms and grand parties, give us hints of what we are doomed for.

The city sounds unique, whether it be a tinny blues record on Maxwell and Halsted, or the thudding of ground hammers beating the ground to death for the sake of another tall building.

And if we really want to refresh ourselves, we must always return to what it tasted like...the snowcones, the hot watermelon slices, the popcorn, the too wet kisses, the hot biscuits with home made butter, the ashes....

The House of Eng

Years ago there was this wonderful Chinese restaurant in Hyde Park, on the penthouse level in the El Prado Hotel.

The place was like a fairy land to me, a spot where I could go to have a well mixed drink, eat an authentic Cantonese meal (no chop suey here), gaze out onto the lake, day dream, get away from the city tensions.

Beautifully designed restaurant, seductively decorated, Chinese style. A long bar at the entrance, huge dining room beyond and a terrace on the northern side for those special moments and special people.

The bartender never seemed to take his nose out of the air (I think it helped make his daiquiris taste better) and the waitresses were lovely, helpful and hip. No matter how often you came with a different person, or how many times you came during the week, they always greeted you as though you were a first time visitor.

I would have fond memories of the House of Eng 'til this day, if for no other reason, than the fact that it's where I last saw Cozette.

What was Cozette's last name? I can't remember. But, it doesn't matter anyway, she's probably been married two or three times since I saw her. Haven't we all?

The thing about Cozette is that we shared a lifestyle, a neighborhood and a kind of love that a few people know about these days.

I met Cozette when we were teenagers living on 44th and Indiana. She was my sister's friend but I soon developed a special relationship with her. It would take a long time to explain what the relationship was because it was more like a feeling than anything else.

I loved her, oh yes, of course, I loved her, I was in love with her, but that was unavoidable. First off, you'd have to love a girl-woman as lovely as she was at fourteen-fifteen.

She was exotic for 44th and Indiana Avenue. If she had placed a ticlak in the center of her forehead and draped a sari around her slender body, she could've been Indira Gandhi's daughter.

We knew she was slightly different but there were no anthropologists measuring heads on 44th Street, no authorities who knew what to tell us about a girl whose mother looked like a Gypsy, who sat on the front porch with bracelets on both arms from elbow to wrist, huge bangled earrings and gaudy skirts that trailed around her ankles and had a brother named Fuad.

Eventually, we discovered that Cozette's family was African-American-Egyptian. But prior to that she was simply this beautiful little slender girl with a smile that made friends out of people who wanted to kick her ass because she had naturally straight black hair, and a profile that should've tipped us off about her connection to the Pyramids.

I grew to love Cozette more and more, the older we got. It wasn't what you'd call a lascivious love. It was a truly romantic love. I can remember days of waiting to see her walking down the street on her bird legs, a full skirt wrapped around her thin body, a luscious glow in her face.

Sometimes we'd walk a block together, or simply talk. Sometimes, while we talked, we'd hold hands. It was like a custom with the two of us, like two people who had designed their own cultural habits.

We, my family, moved from 44th Street, of course, to 39th Street, to 51st Street, to the Westside, to 35th Street, to St. Lawrence, to wherever. But I always managed to figure out a way to see Cozette.

The time frames began to stretch. Sometimes I wouldn't see her for a year, we were off on our journeys. When we did see each other we'd hug and hold onto each other for hours.

We didn't ask each other things like, "Are you married?"

"Where've you been?" "What's happening with your brother/sister?" No none of that stuff. We'd just hold onto each other.

How many of us had survived 44th and Indiana? What the hell was there to ask questions about? If we were alive we knew we had accomplished great things.

The time frame eventually stretched into years. I went half way 'round the world with Cozette on my mind. And returned.

Back in Chicago after skiing in Siberia, running with the bulls in Pamplona, living on the island of Lesbos, freaking out in Germany, wandering thru the Brazilian jungle called Rio de Janeiro, different stuff.

Back in Chicago, the House of Eng. I prepared myself for a couple days before, I went running on the lake front, stayed away from rum n'coke, things like that.

I dressed down for my return to the House; I wanted the food to get the attention, not me. A tiny splash of Sniff-Me-Sweet on both cheeks and I was ready.

The sign in the elevator said "House of Eng." I relaxed a bit. The elevator doors opened and once again it was there for me.

The snooty bartender, the long bar, the soft, red and yellow atmosphere. I was in my groove.

The time was right (3:30 p.m., at least three hours before

the dinner time gang made their appearance).

"I'll have a daiquiri."

He recognized me, of course, but he wasn't into doing recognition scenes, he was into making the best daiquiris in the world. I looked through the arch at the end of the bar, into the cavernous dining room. Mmmmmmmmmmm...

The House of Eng. I sipped the daiquiri and couldn't resist smacking my lips with pleasure. The bartender lowered his nose a half inch and almost smiled.

It was still there, that ambience that money can't create, the elegance that develops when good taste is present. I felt at ease in the place.

The maitre d' put in a discreet appearance at my left shoulder.

"Will you be having dinner with us, sir?"

"Yes, you may reserve a table for me, I'll be in the dining room shortly."

"Whenever you wish, sir."

The lady wore dragon silks and moved like a ghost. She took me back to a cluster of moments. The time I had lunch with this major league beauty who turned out to be a dud.

"Why don't they have chop suey on the menu? I love chop suey."

My dinner with brother Eli, his first civilian meal after ten years of dining at Statesville Penitentiary.

"Damn man, who in the fuck tol' you about this place?"

Any my times alone, when I was privileged to have enough coins in pocket to treat myself to the six course dinner that started with "wonderful egg drop soup" and ended with "delightful lobster."

Looking around, taking it all in. I was almost not surprised to see her sitting on the terrace, a dreamy expression on her face. It seemed so natural that she'd be there.

I resisted the impulse to hop off my stool to rush out and

embrace her, sat still instead and studied her. The Gypsy-Egyptian profile had thickened a smidgeon and she was five pounds heavier on top; Cozette!

Cozette, Cozette, Cozette. I slid off the stool and made my way around the bar, thru the French windows and out onto the terrace.

She looked at me carefully, not showing surprise either, and floated over into my arms. Lord only knows how long we stood there, cinched together.

"I was wondering when I'd see you again, it's been a long time."

"Yes, it has been a long time."

One of the waitresses came out onto the terrace and diplomatically steered us back to Cozette's table.

"Shall I cancel your table inside, sir?"

"Yes, cancel his table"

We had the shy feeling for the first time, but there was still no need to go back to the past for anything, we had that covered. We could take it from now.

"Are you waiting for someone?"

"No, I just decided to take the day off from work and treat myself to dinner at the House."

The hip people always called it "The House."
We smoothly rearranged for me to be seated at her table on the terrace.

The lustrous glow on her face told me everything; she was healthy and happy.

"Cozette, this is July 25, 1991, and I love you do you know that?"

"Yes, I do know that. And do you know that I love you too."

The courses began to arrive while we were telepathically communicating. We touched fingers spooning in our soup, smiled idiotically at each other munching on rumaki and did an ethereal melt down with curried shrimps.

I think I asked her to marry me with a glance, she consented with lowered eyelids and nine months later, gave birth to twin boys.

Naturally, it flowed to an end, that was the beauty of the House Eng service, it didn't stop abruptly by having a uniformed monkey throw a bill in your face. It flowed to an end.

Was it an expensive restaurant? Hard for me to say because everything I experienced there was worthwhile.

Six-thirty p.m. already, the dinner crowd was beginning to surround us. We gently put the twins to bed and took a dreamy walk down the hall to our own bedroom.

"Phil, I have to go now, someone is waiting."

I paid the tab, gave my usual generous tip and stepped into the elevator with Cozette. We hugged going down.

Strange, when I think back on it, how seldom we kissed, and when we did kiss it was like our lips embracing, rather than one of those soap opera head swiveling-tongue twining things.

Tropical Chicago evening, a few desperados on the fringes. I walked her to her car. What was there for us to say?

"I'll always love you, Phil."

"I'll always love you too, Cozette."

And she was gone. I felt tempted to go back up to the House and do it over again, hoping that the process would be the catalyst for her reappearance. But it was crazy to think like that and I let it go.

I haven't seen Cozette since that day, about ten years ago this month, and when I was in Chicago last summer I discovered that the House of Eng had disappeared.

Literally, the place had disappeared. There was no forwarding address, no House of Eng Number Two or any of that, it just didn't exist anymore. I was sick for two days after I made the discovery.

I come to this place about once every other week because it reminds me of the House, a little.

Cozette? I feel certain our paths will cross sometime this year, if I'm lucky.

Black Style

The African-Americans in Chicago must be the most stylish people of African descent anywhere on the planet.

Eurocentrically oriented types are fond of saying, "They're like Parisians." The French should be so lucky.

Maybe if France had a 47th Street and King Drive, an 87th Street, or Cabrini Green, Robert Taylor Homes, a Maxwell Street or any of a number of streets in between where African people parade, they might be able to claim a piece of this.

The parade started thousands of years before the Mayflowers' dregs were vomited onto these holy shores, when African tourists and traders bopped around in Mexican port cities and refused to spend too much time in Minnesota because of the weather.

They left a bunch of hip skulls lying around in Olmec land for future racists to try to discredit.

Some of the Chicago styles hint at supernatural origins; check out the brother in the burgundy and ink black, the sister in deep red and egg yolk yellow, the tall couple in sea blue and cloudy white.

The stuff is so out...

From the depths of the roachiest ghetto to the penthouses of the elite we can be certain that we'll be seeing Black Style...

The question has been the subject for debates amongst the cognoscenti for years, we decided to take it to the people.

The Chicago Sister

Willie Daniels, retired, dedicated whist player.

"O, yeahhh, she does exist and I can tell you all about her. There's a ninety-nine percent chance that she's a Southern-souled woman, people most likely came up from Africa, Mississippi, Ghana, Georgia, Nigeria, Tennessee or Soweto, Alabama, somewhere like that, if you know what I mean? And she got that in her blood.

That city thang is strictly on the surface. Go down half a inch 'n you gon' git some South, I guarantee you that.

I'm not gonna sit here and play true confession with you, but I can tell you some thangs. Back in the good ol' days before people became outrageously violent and filled with diseases that we don't have cures for, there was a type of woman that you couldn't find no where else but 'n Chicago.

She was a woman that was brimming over with love and was sweet as a honeycomb. You could find them in the churches and in the night clubs.

Let me explain that...back then a night club wasn't considered the worse place in the world. People used to go to the clubs to hear Muddy Waters, Howlin' Wolf, Lightening Hopkins and people like that, drink a little beer and get up and go to church the next morning.

In some cases what you'd be listening to was a continuation of what you had heard the night before, musically.

I'm not trying to say that the club was exactly the same

as the church, not by a long shot. In some cases the church was a helluva lot livelier than the club, once the preacher got to preachin' and the sinners got to moanin' 'n the sisters got to singin'.

Yeah sir, I know that there's a creature called the Chicago Sister 'cause I was married to one of 'em for thirty-seven years, Lord rest her soul. You play?''

Carl Freeman, Sociologist/Bachelor

"Well, in my opinion, if there ever was a "Chicago Sister" she went the way of the dinosaur, if I'm to believe what my father and the men from his generation have told me.

The sweetness and generosity of spirit that they talk about is dead. I mean, let's face it, I'm thirty years old, got a decent career going for myself and if I meet sister whose in the same field I'm in, we're apt to become competitors before we become lovers.

And there's a sixty-forty chance that she would win the competition based on the sexist racism that's prevalent these days.

If I meet a lady whose above my head careerwise, she's likely to dismiss me because she's looking for bigger game. And I damn sure ain't going to try to find my soulmate in the Robert Taylor Homes or Cabrini Green.

I don't know who this "Chicago Sister" is. Where can I find one?''

Ardella Harp, high school music teacher—divorced.

"Of course, there's a Chicago Sister, who could possibly doubt that she exists? I'd be invalidating myself if I said she doesn't exist. Who is she, how do you define her?

Well I'm tempted to use some incredibly non-standard English and say—she is me, that's who she be!

Where did she acquire those rare traits that are used to classify a Chicago Sister? It would take more time than you have paper for me to sit here and try to answer that one. And you've clearly got to understand that the answer would only be coming to you from this sister's perspective.

I can, however, be specific about certain general things. I know that might sound contradictory but bear with me.

Number one, the Chicago Sister is always multifaceted. I think that comes from the fact that we have so many different frames of reference. I'm originally from a small town called Chit'lin Switch, in Mississippi.

But I know sisters here from the Caribbean, from Africa, from other sections of the country and I consider them Chicago Sisters.

Number two, Chicago Sisters take care of business. I don't care whether we're talking about Mahalia Jackson, Margaret Burroughs, Oprah Winfrey, Gwendolyn Brooks or Sadie Mae down on the corner, we take care of business.

Number three, we can put some Electric Slide under a brother that will make him feel like he's listening to Earth music.

Need I say more?"

Mavis Brickley, Robert Taylor Projects, four children, drug problem, (crack).

"I don't see no mo' difference between some Black chick from Chicago than I see from New Jersey or Kansas City or anywhere else.

A woman is got it hard, no matter where she at. My ol' man cut out on me midway thru my second pregnancy, okay? He left me with one mouth to feed and another one on the way and a drug habit, okay? Does that make me a Chicago Sister?

What does all this bullshit mean anyway? Seems like that

115

all some people have to do is sit around on they fat asses and try to put labels on other people.

Hey, it snows real hard in Chicago in the winter time and your ass can get real cold. Does that make me a Chicago Sister?

I've had my purse snatched three times this month, lucky I didn't have no money in it. My youngest daughter was raped in the elevator last week. My oldest son is in juvenile home for trying to hold up the corner liquor store and I'm on the edge of losin' my motherfuckin' mind.

Does that qualify me to be a Chicago Sister? And how much do you get anyway, for being a Chicago Sister?''

Dap Sugah Charlie, ex-pimp, Gospel Singer.

"Chicago Sistah? O yes Lawd! I had four of 'em in my stable at one time...ahhem, before I saw the error of my evil ways and reformed.

"During those times, when I was filled up to my neck with sin 'n devilment, I'd tell anybody—gimme a Chicago woman any day. They some strong sistahs. I used to use binoculars to keep tabs on 'em when they were down in the streets, and they'd stand out there in them neon streets for six or eight hours at a time, in sub-zero weather, hustling their tails off.

I didn't let 'em use hot water bottles 'n stuff, the way some pimps did, I'd have 'em wear extra socks.

Money factories, that's what they were. Treacherous and slick too. You always had to stay alert else they'd get the uppers on you. Sistahs had a lot of heart and you had to be a lotta pimp to pimp'em, they'd eat a poot butt pimp up! Like I said, before I saw the error of my ways I took advantage of one of the greatest treasures in this country, the Black Woman, the Chicago Sistah.

"The big distinction I see, now that I've reformed, is that the same sistah who used to turn tricks is alive and well,

116

but can't nobody trick her. Lawd be praised!"

Riley Johnson, Stockbroker, Remy-Martin-Chicago Bulls fanatic.

"Bottom line, you better believe there's a Chicago Sister, or a woman who fits that mystique to a "T."

"My mom was definitely a Chicago Sister. There were four of us at home when Dad died from high blood pressure, diabetes and smoking two packs of cigarettes a day.

"Dad was an ol' fashioned type and had always been the bread winner in our family. Mom was the housewife and mother, pure and simple.

"But when Dad died, she went to work. She had pie sales, did part time house work, catered for parties, sewed, she worked her fingers to the bone to see that we all had what we needed.

"And she put us to work too. She was infinitely patient and tender hearted but she didn't tolerate any slacking. We did what we were told to do, pronto, or else we got slammed.

"She might not have to slam one of us but once a month, but when she slammed you, you were really slammed. I think she's probably responsible for me knowing how to close a deal."

Sarah Gooding, Socialworker, Intellectual.

"My gut reaction to the possibility of there being a Chicago Sister is the same one I had when I visited Cuba (illegally) in the Sixties.

"Remember the Castro-Che Guevara statements and commitment to the birth and development of the New Man?

"The New Man/Woman was going to turn the selfish, mean spirited world around. The New Person is in my mind, like the Chicago Sister, a revolutionary creature.

"The Chicago Sister is a city version of this phenomenon,

117

the socialistic revolutionary who operates in an urban environment. It isn't possible, at this juncture, to determine the direction of her humanistic expansion, but I'm optimistic about the future.

Am I a Chicago sister? I can't say positively that I am, but my spiritual orientation is in that direction.''

Yasmin Idi Amin, owner, the Afro-Shoppe, Super Nationalist, author of "The Black Woman's Right to be Wrong."

"There's no doubt in my mind that the so-called Chicago Sister is a product of the dominant culture's fantasy, a white man's pipe dream, in other words, just about everything we've been taught to think, to believe about African women from Chicago and African women in general stems from a complete misunderstanding of the Black man's true nature.

If Black men in Chicago were allowed to truly have dominance over his woman, the very idea of a "Chicago Sister" would be repugnant.

Yes, I'm saying repugnant because I don't really think the brothers in Chicago, or anywhere else, want to have to compete with his woman, to be put down by her, to have her turn their children against him, to be forced to deal with a creature whose nature is false.

The true nature of a sister demands that she find her niche in the Black man's scheme of things. We have to remember that the Black man is a king of this world, and the sister is a queen.

I don't see the Chicago sister as a queen because most of them run their mouths too much. Queens are strong and silent and they know their place.

My definition of a "Chicago Sister" is a Black woman out of control. "What the Chicago Sister needs is a fully stocked kitchen and a backhanded slap to the mouth."

118

Jeff Stoneham, Artist, Chauvinist.

"Yeahhh, I am the baddest motherfucker in this city and I'll go one on one with anybody. Let's face it, how many brothers do you know who can take a piece of steel and turn it into a bouquet of roses?

"Or work some faces into porcelain that look like the past and the future. I'm an artist, I can take anything and do art with it.

"The Chicago Sister? Shit! I made the Chicago Sister what she is. Yeah me, that's what you got to look at, strong brothers like me.

"I don't know who said it first, maybe it was me, yeah, it probably was me that said, 'You can tell who the father is from the way the children behave.'

"That's the way it is with a woman, you can tell a lot about the man in a woman's life from the way she behaves.

"I don't try to beat a sister down or nothing like that, but in order for a sister to have a successful relationship with me she's got to know her place.

"I'm the man and she's the woman, that's what we have to have straight from the git. See, that's the thing a lotta brothers get confused about here in Chicago.

"That's the main thing, you can't be confused about yourself. I guarantee you there's always gon' be a Chicago Sister 'long as you got brothers out there like me."

Freddy Harris, night club comedian.

"O hell yes! Gimme a Chicago Sister any day of the week and twice on Sunday. Ain't no doubt in my mind when the good Lawd was creatin' them plastic witches in "EL-A" and those iron maidens in New York, he took a rest in Chicago and liked what was happenin' so much he stayed long enough to create the Chicago Sister.

"My guess is that He waited 'til early summer so that the

sisters wouldn't have to wear winter coats, that way when brothers passed by they'd have a good chance to check out all that pretty butter on them hips and thighs.

"As most of y'all know I'm originally from Quebec, Canada, where most of the Black women are Eskimos. What I'm sayin' is that you got some cold sisters up there. Maybe it's got something to do with being so close to Detroit.

"In any case, the term "Chicago Sister" strikes a chord in my brain, you know what I mean? And they come in all colors 'n shades, a lil bit like BeyBey's children.

"Three years ago I was real close to a sister that had skin the color of a banana, two years ago I was tight with a sister who had this beautiful plum-black color.

"Shit! What the fuck can I say about the Chicago Sister? They come in all kinds of shapes, sizes 'n shades, and if you ain't never spent the winter with one of 'em, yo' life has been a cold ass experience."

Martha J. BenHawk, Teacher, mother of two.
"Listen to me closely. I'm not going to repeat myself. The transportation system in Chicago is as responsible as anything I can think of for creating the Chicago Sister.

"Let me explain; in a lot of cities, lets take Los Angeles, for example, you're the victim of the bus lines, (if you don't have a car) and the bus lines are really what determines what your social status is. Sounds crazy, huh? But that's the way things are.

"In Chicago you can live in Cabrini Green and take a cab or a bus to one of the swank joints and no on will ever know the difference.

"You might have to play a little Cinderella, if you do live in the projects, or have one of the other unpopular addresses (picture any address you can think of on the Near Southside or the Near Westside) but lets face it, nothing is perfect.

"The point I'm trying to make is that the transportation system has created a multifaceted creature (interesting word isn't it? 'multifaceted') who knows how to go up and down, back and forth.

"The transportation system isn't perfect but it has helped in the development of a woman who doesn't feel limited by how far she can go on the Dan Ryan, she can always transfer."

Fred 15X, Muslim, Entrepreneur.

"I have to think that the Hawk is what makes a Chicago Sister what she is, Allah Be Praised, who is responsible for all things . . .

"Nobody can tell me that you wouldn't be a Super Sister, struggling thru snowdrifts and all of that, 'specially an African woman, if you didn't have the help of a Superior element behind you.

"We have to remember that we didn't come from snow, we came from the sun. Now then, for an African woman to make that kind of adjustment, genetically, psychologically, is awe inspiring, 'specially in Chicago, where it can get colder, on many levels, than anywhere in the world."

Debbie Ujima Payne, sorority sister, vegetarian, late twenties.

"I don't feel comfortable with labels like that. What does that link me with? A sister who prepares a breakfast of high cholesterol bacon 'n eggs? Or someone who thinks an idea of a good time is a scotch 'n soda?

"I think it's labels like that that inspire some people to think that African-American sisters are immune to heartache, that we can bear up under any kind of problem.

"This is stereotype stuff. "The Chicago Sister." What's that? What do I have in common with a sister whose idea

121

of giving her children a nutritious meal starts with KOOLAID?

"I am a Chicago Sister because I grew up here. I ate the overcooked Negro food, I survived the "Black is Beautiful" label (yes, I am darker than your average telephone), and watched us lose Washington to Daley, and yes, I can identify with the Chicago Sister, but only if she eats her veggies."

Melvin Simmons, bartender, The Other Place.

"Chicago Sisters?! You just missed them! There were four of 'em sittin' here a few minutes ago. Oh yes, there is such a thing as a Chicago Sister, I'm married to one of them.

"The thing about what makes the sister so unique is real complicated, real complicated. You've got a lot of different threads runnin' thru that cloth.

"Some of the sisters can be a real pain in the ass, some of 'em can be a cure for the pain in the ass. Dig where I'm comin' from?

"I mean, some of the sisters can be so evil at times, but then we got some others who are sweet as honey. They come up in here all the time.

"Let me give you an example; sister comes in here regular, carries a briefcase, wears pinstriped suits a lot, her basic drink is a vodka martini. I get the impression she's under a lot of pressure.

"She can come in here four evenings in a row, sit up here purrin' like a pussy cat and then, on the fifth evening, for some reason she'll come in here and nothing will be right...the music is wrong, there's too much smoke, and I put too much vermouth in her martini, its like she dealing with PMS or something.

"And then, the following day, she'll be right back at her sweet self again. I've learned how to go with the flow. One last thing, don't cross the Chicago Sister, no sir, don't cross 'em. We had a sister come up in here last month 'n shoot a dude who messed over her six years ago. I guess she just started thinking about it and decided to do something...

Rum 'n coke with a wedge of lime? You got it!''

Jamilla Drake, student, track star (100 yard dash, 400 meter relay) Gemini/Virgo rising.

"I can't really say if there is a "Chicago Sister" or not, because I haven't been to any other place, so I wouldn't know with whom to compare her.

"Am I a Chicago Sister? Well, I was born here and I've lived here all of my life. Does that make me a Chicago Sister?''

Ashun DuValier, International Law, Linguist (French, Spanish, Italian, German, Greek, Russian, Yoruba) UN Consultant.

"Yes, there is definitely a Chicago Sister, and I'm one of them, I'm proud to say. I've been to just about every major city in Europe, Africa and South America, including a few island cities, my husband is originally from Port-au-Prince, Haiti, and I never feel totally at ease until I get back here.

"I think it has something to do with a sisterhood I feel with the women I grew up with. We know each other's parents, we've partied together, shared secrets, seen a lot of stuff go down. No matter where I go in the world I always feel close to this.''

Robert J. Fox, politician.

"Well, I never called the girls I grew up with Chicago Sisters, but I guess that's what they've become...''

David Mosshed, student, Cancerian.

123

"I'd have to say yeahh, yeah, there's a "Chicago Sister" and her name is Jamilla Drake, Gemini, Virgo rising..."

Adesina Adelabu, Iyalosha of Ogun.
"If the Chicago Sister didn't exist we'd have to invent her, wouldn't we?"

Bo', a Matador of the Night

If Bo' had been born in Spain he would've been a Manolete; Manolete, a legendary figure of the bullring who developed the art of using only a few passes with the capote (the large cape) and the muleta (the small cape), each pass performed with surgical precision.

We have seen Bo-Manolete enter the arenas of the night calmly moving thru the mob with sandunga and temple' (English equivalents would be confidence and determination), the sounds of invisible trumpets and cheers trailing in his wake.

During his picador-movements, drawing blood from the brave bulls, his sensitivity allowed him to merge his psyche with the beast making the charge, pushing his lance in far enough to wound but not to cripple.

We have seen him lure the night into the correct position for the banderillas with a quick feint to the left, or to the right, plant the sticks where they are supposed to be planted and ease away without a backward glance.

His faena, those series of interwoven movements with the muleta, have taken place across 2:00 a.m. restaurant tables, in fast cars driven on the lake front at 3:00 a.m., on swank bar stools around the world, in the midnight beds of African queens.

And finally, because the bullfight must end, as in life, with Death, we have watched him make the kill with his ears.

125

While many other matadors hustle to kill for the ears, and tail, he has often made the kill with his ears (or eyes), listening and watching the night to death.

While others frantically swirl their capes, do dances of frenzy, beg approval from the crowd and stab at the bull with nervous emotions, Bo quietly positions the night with a careful nod of the head or meaningful look and, at the moment of Truth, delicately slips his point into a vital spot, going straight in over the horn, the way its supposed to be done.

After the kill we've never seen him stand over the body, bragging about his greatness. The feeling he has given us, at the break of day, is one of harmony with the night, an animal that must be slaughtered to make way for the morning. Bo', a matador-lover of the night, never kills for the sake of killing. If he had been born in Spain he would've been a Manolete.

Chicago-Madrid

I was sitting in the old bullring in Madrid, one chilly afternoon, people around us sipping twenty-five peseta shots of sherry from the vendor, when the thought hit me.

What the fuck am I doing here, in Madrid, at the corrida? Me, a Chicago born and bred brother from the 'hood. I turned to my lady with the question on the tip of my tongue, canceled it when I saw how absorbed she was. Or was it the sherry?

The question fixed itself on my brain. For an hour and a half I watched and listened to the bullfights in Chicago (they were broadcast from Mexico, sometimes from Spain) as Chamaco, Diego Puerta, Paco Camino, Manole Vasques, Juan "Bilboa" Montes, and someone who called himself "El Voluntario" fought huge bulls in front of me, merging with images of past fights on TV.

Was I hallucinating?

The six bulls and men fighting in front of me were dedicating the afternoon to the memory of Antonio Bienvenida, a courageous matador from an earlier time who had blown the horn on the hornshavers, the act of a man of honor and integrity.

The hornshavers were an unscrupulous bunch of people who sought to distort the bull's thrusts by shaving their horns, the effect would be the same as shortening a boxers' left jab by two inches.

The weird thing about the practice, which was supposed to give the bullfighter an advantage, is that it didn't work too well. There were just as many men gored by bulls whose horns had been shaved as there were by bulls whose horns hadn't been shaven.

In Chicago, in the 60s, when I became an aficionado I didn't know anything about horn shaving, Miuras, Madrid, or a thousand other bits of esoterica connected to the corrida.

Strange, I thought, in between oles!, the paths that lead us from there to here. The path for me had its beginning in the Drake Hotel kitchen.

I was a delivery boy-soda fountain helper who was sent to pick up supplies from the kitchen periodically. Fascinating place, the Drake Hotel kitchen. It was as large as a medium sized town and had the most interesting bunch of people I'd ever met.

One of my favorites was a Mexican cookie baker who looked like Cantiflas, and was proud of it.

He was one of those rare people who could tell a joke in any language and make you laugh, or simply cock his mustache in a certain way and lay you in the aisle. Hell, he could've been Cantiflas, for all I know.

What made him give me the ticket? Who knows? Maybe I had stolen something from the drugstore and given it to him, I was prone to do stuff like that.

"Hey, hombre, you ever been to dee bullfight?"

"Naw, I ain't never been to no bullfight."

I had heard about them of course, I lived on the Southside and we had heard about everything on the Southside.

The movie ticket was for the Old World Playhouse (the art theatre on Michigan Avenue, near Roosevelt University) and it was the screening of a grainy film featuring Manolete. My friend had dropped me off on the top of the mountain.

The grizzled old Cuban cigar smokers sitting around me

who were not screaming olé each time a bullfighter changed his muleta from hand to hand reminded me of the audience I had shared my filmed intro to the bullfight.

I was hooked from the first time. If it had been heroin I would be a dope fiend right now, thirty some years later.

I left the theatre feeling as though I had been privileged to be a part of a great Ritual.

Where could I find another Ritual, how could I reaffirm my—whatever had happened?

(Bullfights, live or filmed, were in short supply in Chicago then and now.)

Chamaco, back in Madrid, was performing a left-handed, natural dripping the muleta so skillfully in front of the bulls nose that he gave the illusion of having the bull smell the hemline of the cloth.

The old men around me straightened up slightly, one of them blew a soft funnel of smoke in the direction of the fight.

My introduction was not confirmed immediately, it was years later. In between times I stared at pictures of fighting bulls wherever I could find them, and read like a maniac.

As a matter of fact, I had become a maniac. It was a wild situation. I was hooked on something that didn't exist in the place where I lived.

Months would pass before I'd have another "real" fix (I didn't consider the pictures and books "real").

A "real" fix was "The Life of Luis Procuna," a Mexican matador who was the bravest and most cowardly of a great heritage of brave cowards.

I went to see "Procuna" every day for two weeks, staying for the second showing a few days.

Chamaco profiled, sighted down the channels of the blade and took the bull onto his sword as though he were plunging into a brown mound of horned butter.

The bull dropped as though he had been blessed with a

thunderbolt. A couple of the old men nodded approval and two grunted olé.

People in my neighborhood looked at me funny. I was the dude going around looking for a bullfight.

"Hey, man, have you ever been to the bullfight?"

I managed to get married, still looking for the bullfight.

"Baby, you know what we have to do, we have to go to Spain, to see the bullfight."

Chamaco did a quick turn of the ring. This was the day to be as superior as you could be, but not to hog the audience, give that to the memory of Antonio Beinvenida.

Diego Puerta followed Chamaco, looking serious as he knelt in front of the gate where the bull would charge into the ring.

Well, as we all know, you can get what you want if you want it badly enough, 'specially in Chicago. The bullfights were being shown on Channel 34, on Wednesday night.

I forget who told me or how I found out, but my soul had been saved. Channel 34? Who 'n the fuck has it?

Nick had it, that's who had it and that's where I went to see it.

Diego Puerta was taking the bull away from the picador after two pics. He was doing the beautiful chicuelina antigua, wrapping himself in the capote like a dressing gown.

Nick didn't give a shit about it and his wife didn't pay the spectacle any mind. I wound up sharing one hour of the corrida every Wednesday night with his mother-in-law and a well bred Boxer, who knew a good thing when he saw it.

I'm going to call her Miss Essie, the mother-in-law, and Chongo the Boxer. Miss Essie shuffled past the room where I was glued to the TV, she stood there for a spell with a soft drink full of Seagram 7 and, without a word, hunkered down on the sofa nearby.

"Well, well, will you look at this?! A man wavin' a red

flag in front of a full grown bull. He's gonna git his drawers in shreds if he ain't careful."

We saw Diego Puerta in better form on TV than when I caught him in Madrid. Miss Essie had espanolized herself to the point of being able to pronounce Spanish names, to a point.

"Look at that, wid a bull like that Dee-a-go Puta oughta be able to do a better fay-na than that."

Chongo always erected his ears at the moment of Truth, as though he were hearing sounds none of us could hear.

It went on for weeks, months; my wife accused me of having dates with another woman on Wednesday nights after I'd talked so much about Miss Essie.

"A lot of clever men do that, you know? They talk about the other woman in their lives as though she were legit, you know what I mean?"

Diego Puerta performed an honest day's labor with what turned out to be a pedestrian bull and now it was Paco Camino's turn.

My woman took up the challenge, she agreed to accompany me to the Wednesday night scene. Lucky sister, it was the night they showed Aruzza dismounting to do what only he could do in the arena.

Billy never questioned where I was going on Wednesday night after she saw Aruzza (who had been semi-officially retired) perform four aruzzinas and a mesmerizing pendulo' on a bull that was as tall as a horse.

She didn't want to go see this stuff every Wednesday, but she acknowledged, "that's some deep shit."

Manolo Vasques, Juan "Bilbao" Montes and the weirdo who called himself "El Voluntario" tried to give each other "the bath," but they were overshadowed by an evening with Manuel Capetillo, Luis Dominquin, Antonio Ordonez, Armillita, Alfredo Leal and the shadows of Joselito,

131

Belmonte and El Gallo.

I couldn't scream "oles!" enthusiastically, not with the televised memories of those legends in the back of my skull. I swiveled my neck around to take a closer look at the old Cuban cigar smokers. They were perched on the edges of the stone seats as though they were afraid to get too comfortable. Some of them leaned on carved canes, they all had the look of the past in their eyes.

We often had that look, I imagine, Miss Essie, Chongo and myself, after an evening of staring at the majestic movements of the greatest bullfighters ever televised.

I Go Come...

"You got to go away from here and come back to really understand what time can do. You prop your high school album open and stare at all these shining black, brown, beige and ivory shaded faces and re-design the scenarios that you once shared.

The brother named King Johnson, who really looked and behaved like a King. Judy Frazier, the perfect high school girl, pep team leader, student body president, destined for the major leagues.

Fenster MacRoy, class comedian, a delightful person with whom to open the day. Carmen Tolliver, the prettiest girl in the album (some people would vote for Margaret Appliney), snooty as hell and so full of herself you couldn't even talk to her unless your hair was curly.

Phillip Harrison, the "egghead." Oleana Bradshaw, the country girl from Mississippi, who made straight A's for her last two years in school.

Bobby Truman, the baddest 100 yard man who ever ran it. You look at the album and try to imagine what they are like now...that's why you have to go away and come back.

Thats what they say a lot in Ghana—"I go come."

I Go Come Back

Forrestville School had some shadows in it that night that will never be seen again and a full moon that was a waxy face. Karen lifted up her blouse and invited me to kiss her breasts.

"Go 'head, Jimmy, kiss 'em, make me feel good."
I stared at them for a long time. Karen's breasts were so beautiful. They weren't big like a lot of the other girls, but they were perfectly shaped pears with blueberries in the center.
I made both of us feel good. How old were we? Fourteen-fifteen? Hormones were driving us like slave cylinders and the soft-sappy winds that fan passion in the spring, in Chicago...were everywhere.

Karen was perfect for me that Spring-Summer. Nothing meant anything, no one else mattered but Karen. I went to sleep dreaming about her and woke up thinking about her. I still think a lot about her.

She lived a half block from Forrestville and had strict parents, which meant that she could only steal an hour or so with me whenever.

I had to be ready always.
"I don't know if I can make it tomorrow evenin', Jimmy but if I can it'll be at 9:15."

I was there at 8:15. I was so feverish about her and she was so romantic.

"Jimmy, look up there. What do you see?"

"I see stars, baby, but I also see a star down here."

She was food, music, art, strength, vision and one night in July she became satisfaction.

We had kissed and fondled each other to the point of tactile madness over the course of May and June. It was July 9th and she had managed to steal an hour (9:30—10:30, at her "girlfriends house") for us to share.

"How did you know I was goin' to be able to get away?"

"I don't know, I could just feel it in my bones."

Tropical Chicago, a breeze shifts a single leaf and dissolves. We wedged ourselves together in the doorway at the rear of the school, yards of school gravel and other couples meeting filled in the distance.

Karen was so natural, so warm and sweet. I had the feeling that every bone in her body met mine, every push against her was met by the right counterpush.

"Jimmy, do you want to?"

I held her so tight I must've mashed the breath out of her.

"You know I do baby."

"Go 'head do what you wanna do."

She moved a few inches away from me and pulled the front of her skirt up. She didn't have any panties on. I tried to be as suave as possible trying to reach down inside a pair of tight blue jeans to pull out an engorged penis.

"Karen, what happens if you get pregnant?"

Her eyes looked like full moons and her voice was so low she sounded like a woman.

"I don't care, I love you, Jimmy."

Somebody a whole lot wiser than me will have to explain why I just didn't plunge right in and fuck up.

"I love you, Jimmy" may have struck a chord.

I wedged my dick between her tight young thighs on her clitoris and masturbated us to a climax.

135

"Oh, Jimmy," she moaned when she felt me pump a summer's worth of cum between her legs. "Oh, Jimmy." she shivered.

She leaned back from me on unsteady legs, holding her dress up like a Can-Can dancer. Both of us stared at our cum sliding down her thighs (a friend from later years called it "Love Snot") in the moon light.

"Jimmy, you didn't put it inside of me." She spoke as though a miracle had happened, and embraced me.

Years later, at a conference in Oakland, California (The role of the African-American woman in Contemporary life) Karen stood in front of me and saluted.

"Captain Karen DuMangier, at your service!"

We smiled and laughed and hugged each other for fifteen minutes before we could talk.

"What's this Captain stuff?"

"That's my retirement rank, I've just spent twenty years in the military. What've you been up to?"

We diced that up a few ways and took the elevator up to her room to talk.

"Jimmy, make yourself a drink, I want to change into something more comfortable."

The Hyatt Regency Hotel in Oakland, California is a helluva shot from Forrestville School. I poured myself a small cognac and settled myself into the standard hotel room sofa.

Karen Delphine DuMangier, Army Captain? I shook my head in disbelief. What the hell had happened to take her from where we had been in the Forrestville School yard to being a Captain in the Army?

I sipped my cognac and stared out of the window. A full moon stared back at me. I smiled at the memory of the times we shared. The sister looked good.

It was obvious that her twenty years stint in the Military

had kept her in good shape. I patted my flat stomach and made a silent vow to commit myself to more health club hours.

I subconsciously raised my glass to toast her when she made a gorgeous-naked appearance in the bathroom doorway.

She leaned against the door frame, a Mona Lisa smile on her mouth, and folded her arms under her beautiful breasts. They weren't pears anymore, they had become cantaloupes and I felt my mouth suddenly water.

She held her arms out to me..."Jimmy, I think I owe you something..."

I carefully placed my drink on the cocktail table and moved toward her, the thought of that old saying buzzing in my head..."the melon you wait the longest for is often the sweetest."

I go come back.

"Romona Spelling?! Ramona Spelling?! Isn't that Ramona Spelling?"

"Looks like her."

Fred and I stared at the heavy bottomed woman with the mountainous breasts doing a down ' dirty on the dance floor with a brother who was clearly overmatched.

She was wedged into a blood red dress and her head was obviously smoky.

A rivulet of perspiration flowed from her face and neck, down the tightly bunched cleavage. The sister was hot.
She loved to dance, you could see that from the way she used the music. And she was good. Her hips went one way, her breasts the opposite way as she flung her head back and flailed the smoky air with her arms.

Romona Spelling. I glanced at Fred's profile.

"Y'all had a thang goin on fer awhile, didn't you?"
He stared at the woman doing obscene gyrations on the dance

137

floor and took a long sip on his drink.

"Yeahhh, we had a heavy number going on for two years, from, July 1990 to July 1992."

"It must've really been a thang for you to remember it that precisely."

"Yeahhh, it was," he answered slowly. Fred wasn't the kind of brother who ran his mouth a lot. Ramona had found a new way to clench and unclench her buttocks in time to the beat.

A wild eyed type strolled past us mumbling to the general public . . . "that sister got a helluva turd cutter on 'er! A helluva turd cutter!"

The blast of the music ended for a few counts before going on to a slower piece, a bona fide Chicago belly rubber. Ramona Spelling grabbed her partner's arm as he tried to lead her off the floor, spun him around and plastered her thighs against his thighs.

"C'mon, man, lets see what's happenin' at Reese's." Fred and I, friends since high school, were doing a number that brothers on the southside do quite often. You get together for an evening of evaluating the current talent.

The Other Place had been the third stop of the night. It was 1 AM and Reese's would probably be the last stop of the night. We were pleasantly high.

The brother seemed a bit preoccupied as he drove thru the friday night streets.

"Damn! Of all the people to see, why would it have to be her?"

I was staring out of the passenger's side at a trio of lovely Black women getting out of a Mercedes.

"Who? Who you talking about?"

They looked like jungle birds in their electric oranges, bright greens, slashes of red and burgundy, I could almost smell the perfumes from their gorgeous bodies as we drove past.

"Ramona."

We managed to get a space in the crowded parking lot and started the slow stroll toward the club. Fred wanted to talk about Ramona, I could tell. I decided to give him the opening.

"What happened between you two?"

Reese's is in a lively mood. The bartender was leading a section of the bar in a Happy Birthday song, several couples were having animated talks at both bars (Reese's split down the middle during the summer of '91), people were having the kind of good time that gives the atmosphere a sparkling feeling.

Mrs Burnside was on the scene, as usual, chitchatting with friends and making certain that the festivities were kept within reasonable bounds.

"Hi ya doin', Anna?

"Hi Fred, Jimmy, how're you guys doin'?"

We captured a couple seats and ordered Martell . . .

"What happened between us?"

We had to turn for a serious look at two wonderfully designed sisters making a slow parade to the dance area-bar in the rear. Chicago has the finest collection of African-American women in the country, and most of them know it, thats why they walk the way they do.

"Well, first of all, I'm not goin' to take you back into ancient history or anything but you remember Ramona from high school?"

"Shit, I remember Ramona from Wilson Junior College."

"O.K., think back to the way she was then and contrast that with what you saw tonight."

The contrast was easy to make. Ramona Spelling in high school was traditional version of Miss Goodie Two Shoes. She didn't kiss, wouldn't allow you to slide your hand down on her boody (if you got a chance to slow dance with her,if),

139

would back away from a dirty story and went to church every Sunday.

"Yeah, man she is different now. What happened?"

"I can't righteously say, all I can tell is that I was there when it happened."

I exchanged flirtatious looks with a beige colored school teacher three seats away. We reinforced it by checkin' each other in the bar mirror.

"I wouldn't want anybody to take this as gospel but I'd have to say the change happened right after we had sex for the third time."

The beige colored lady flickered her eyelashes correctly. She knew how to flirt...hmmmmmmmm....

"The third time?"

"Thats right, the third time we had a terrible time the first two times, the chick was a semi-virgin. I think the farthest she had ever gone was to let some motherffucker finger fuck her."

We locked eyes in the mirror for a pregnant moment. She was telling me all I wanted to know; I'm here for a drink, I'm pretty, intelligent, driving a nice car, got a career and I'm feeling seductive. Who are you?

There is lots to be said in a bar mirror if you know the language.

"How was I suppose to know that I had discovered a cum freak?"

"Cum freak? Ramona Spelling? You gotta be kiddin'."

The bartender paused in front of us, took the nod and gave us refills.

"Don't ask me how it happened, all I know is that it happened. Like I said, the first two times I almost skinned the head off my dick but after that we were off to the races.

The first inkling I had that the sister was a sex fiend happened one night after a trip to the lake front. Real hot

140

night, we had gone down to Buckingham Fountain, you know, to cool out.

On the way back she persuaded me to drive thru Washington Park.

"Fred, Fred," she says to me, "lets go out into the middle of the big field 'n do it."

I called the bartender over.

"Scuse me, Fred...uhhh, I see that the lady three seats to my right needs a refill, would you do that with my compliments?"

I wanted to hear about Fred and Ramona but I didn't want to lose the beige queen in the process.

"Go on, man..."

He checked my possibility out.

"Yeahhhh, she nice. Anyway, I didn't need too much persuasion to do what she wanted because, well, if the truth be told, the girl had some sho' 'nuff good stuff, you know what I mean?"

Me and the lady held up our snifters to exchange toasts. We were going to be a class act, I could tell, I checked my watch—1:35am—I'd make a slow move in her direction in a few minutes.

"It got to be real crazy after that, real crazy. Her big kick was outdoor fuckin. It got to the point where I was damned near afraid to take her anywhere.

And then she started gainin weight 'n stuff because she discovered marijuana. I think one of her girlfriends turned her on. If I saw her on Friday, we wouldn't do nothin but get high, fuck, eat and do it again all weekend.

And then she started gettin gross, you know, cussin' 'n shit..."

I could tell that the school teacher was becoming impatient. What was more important, the conversation I was having with this bearded hard leg, or the conversation I was going

141

to have with her?

"So y'all broke up, huh?"

"I think the best way to put it is to say that I broke away. I had to. You know what this chick proposed?"

"Naw, What?"

"She proposed that I get some of my friends together, and she'd get some of her friends together and we'd have a fuck out. Can you imagine somebody proposing some shit like that in 1992?"

"Hard to imagine," I replied and checked the time. 1:50 AM. They'd be turning the lights on in ten minutes and calling out, "Last call for alcohol, last call."

"Yeahhh, hard to imagine."

"Anyway, thats what happened. You better get on over there before the lady decides to ease out.

"Been checking us out, huh?"

"It was gonna be you or me."

We shook hands as I slid off the barstool and eased into vacant one next to Madame Beige.

"Good evening, my name is James Bennet."

"My name is Ellen Barlow, my friends call me Billie, for some strange reason."

"What should I call you?"

"Are you a friend?"

"I hope to be."

"Last call for alcohol, last call!"

The bartender placed two Martells in front of us.

"Compliments of the brother."

Fred was wishing us success. The lady and I smiled and toasted him.

"Nice friend you have," she said.

I nodded in agreement.

"Well looks like this is going to be the end of a brief friendship, unless you'll give me your phone number?

"I'm confused. Is your pumpkin going to turn into a rat or something?"

"No , nothing like that, I'm riding with my friend."

She gave me a shy look. She had marvelous cat eyes and dimples in her cheeks. I was hooked.

"I can give you a lift, if you're not afraid to be out with someone you just met."

It was my turn for the sly smile. If she hadn't made the offer I would've been a mad ass.

"You're someone I just met that I feel I've known before."

"Thats a nice thing to say."

"Scuse me, let me tell my friend that I have a lift."

"Hope you're not anxious to rush right home," she whispered, "I like to take walks in the park early in the morning."

I winked lasciviously.

The lights were on and we were strolling out of the club.

"Fred, I got a lift from this lovely lady. Ellen Barlow, Fred Frazier." Fred gave his look of approval, she smiled neutrally.

We started across the street into the parking lot. Fred edged up behind me and whispered in my left ear.

"If you wind up in the park with her, you might have a Ramona Spelling on your hands!"

I was still smiling when I popped into her black BMW. If she was a Ramona Spelling she had picked on the right man this 2 am.

Yeahhh, you got to go away from here and come back to really understand what time can do. 'member King Johnson, the brother who looked and behaved like a king?

King runs a successful funeral home over there on Cottage Grove. Some people say he's into a little drug dealing, but we haven't seen any proof.

Judy Frazier, right here in the album, with the white ruffled collar, the perfect high school girl," the student body president and all that. Well, she did exactly what everybody thought she was gonna do, the problem is that she's married to a piece of po' white trash who flushes her money down the drain.

How did she wind up with po' white trash? Who knows what the egg is gonna have in it?

Fenster MacRoy, class comedian, is playing 'Vegas. Some people think that he's funnier than Richard Pryor was in his day.

Carver Tolliver went out to the west coast and is trying to break into the movies. You gotta give it to the girl, she is persistent

Phillip Harrison, the "egghead," owns his own computer firm. Oleana Bradshaw, the country girl from Mississippi who made straight A's for her junior and senior year, went back down to the big foot country and became a politician. I read somewhere that they're talking about having her run for governor.

Wouldn't that be a kick in the head?

Bobby Truman, the baddest 100 yard man who ever ran it couldn't out run the police, he's doing fifteen years in Statesville.

Wonder what ever happened to the white boy and his sister who went to Du Sable when it was all black? What am I saying? It's always been all Black.

Grits, the Spiritual Side

People in Chicago, transplanted southerners whose ancestors were transplanted, can get real serious about their grits.

"No ma'am, I don't eat no watery grits."

"Uhh, 'scuse me, Miss Lady, but would you please take these back? Too much salt."

We have folks who are partial to their grits with too much salt, just to keep the balance here. And people who only want country fresh butter or hot grits with sugar, butter or not with sugar, butter and milk. And others who love steak gravy or cheddar cheese or bacon grease poured on top.

Why grits? 'cause its fufu in another form. What's fufu? Its pre-American grits.

Greasin'...A Guest Review
by Be'Helthi

Years ago in the southside ghetto and on the westside (we say "on the westside" and "on the southside") you could find the worst food to eat on the planet. And unmercifully, things haven't changed very much.

It would take a historian (we say "ourstorian") to explain how we got into this nutritional insane asylum. That's not my job. I'm simply going to be taking a hard look at some of the components.

Now then, we had a good time at the Play Time, made a date in the Dating Game, swept thru my Place and the Other Place, made lightening creeps into the President's Lounge (checked Chazz out), The Apartment, Piece of the Rock, Reese's, The 50 Yard Line, The Dew Drop Inn, The Palm Garden, and a few other spots no one knows about but us.

Dawn streaks beckon the sky to get hot again (its summer, ain't it?) as our stomachs rumble.

"Hey y'all, why don't we have breakfast?"

The Breakfast Place (name changed to protect the guilty) is open to serve us as much cholesterol as we can bear.

"How do you want your eggs?"

"I'd like cheddar sprinkled on my grits."

"I don't know about y'all but I want some butter on my grits."

Bacon, eggs, hamburgers, steaks, sugar and cream every

where. We waddled out after the breakfast ("break-fast") guts filled with cholesterol, high blood pressure catalysts, diabetes yeast start ups, grease for the future.

And...ahhh, a smoke after the breakfast, doing whatever is necessary to ensure bad health for the next generation what do we need with crack?

Years ago, yes, you can say that if you're older than thirty years ago, I ate the candy corn Spanish peanuts and washed it down with Coca Cola. We sucked on giant peppermint sticks in dill pickles (girls did that a lot) and developed an unbelievable number of cavities.

One of the things I notice now is that many of our sisters paid for feeding on candy bars and sugar filled chewing gum. But we're getting off the track, then was then, Now is Now. Now we go to the swanky named restaurants ("Nom de Plume") where they would kick you out if you ordered grits or chit'lins, but they serve, in crude European imitation style, iced wine.

"And how is your wine, sir?"

"Its frozen, how can I tell how it is."

"Beg pardon, sir?"

"Forget it, put the bottle on the table, maybe we can thaw it out before the night is over."

"As you wish, Sir."

The customer is always right, you see.

They say to me, "Be'Helthi, we have this wonderful new restaurant for you, come with us ." And I go because I'm a gopher, o.k.? and what do I find?

I find a pretentiously attended establishment (my coined slang for a snobbish hang out) where pasta is post dente ("al dente" doesn't mean shit to the middle echelon types who support these places), the vegetables have been desecrated by overcooking and the meat (gotta have a "meat" cooked, baked broiled, fried to within an inch of...well, what? Its

147

already dead.

Chicken is reserved for a special brand of crucifixion, a misfried, over battered or barbequed fate that seems perfectly suited for a bird who has been worked to death and flung into the ghetto for consumption.

Barbecue. Some evening in the summer when the wind is blowing right, I feel that every pig and cow's ribs in the state of Illinois is being charcoaled. And why? I ask myself; so that the brothers and sisters on the southside and on the westside will have some flesh to accompany their macaroni and potato salad (loaded with mayonnaise).

The fast food corporation took note of our predilection for monotonous diets a while back (they didn't believe we'd dig it 30 years ago) and played into it. How else could you explain why a woman or a man would eat those little hamburgers all the time.

The African people in Chicago will use any excuse to eat the worst food in the world (we're not talking about the Be'Helthi conscious people). Christmas Day offers a prime example.

Yeahhh, I know, Be'Helthi is just a dirty rotten snake-dog-motherfucker-bastard-asshole-son of a bitch!

"Christmas! He's talkin' against Christmas! He must be a communist or a white boy!

Sorry, just an African-American man with permanent affiliations for what goes into our bellies. Christmas, what do I have to say beyond pies cakes and those little specialties that we're never able to diet off after Christmas?

The New Year's Day Feast in front of "The Game."

As the sign on the t-shirt says, "Shit happens."

Some folks are starting to talk up a Martin Luther King Festival Feast for his birthday, January 21st.

We're already into some green stuff on St. Patrick's Day, this is for Africans with Irish monikers.

Easter takes our children deeply into those egg-sized chocolates and candy things, Lord knows what the connection is between eggs, rabbits and Jesus reborn.

But then, I'm only a social critic of the African-American food scene, what do I know?

I know there's some kind of manic logic happenin' behind the idea of taking overweight, high blood pressure ridden diabetic mammas to high cholesterol feasts on Mother's Day.

"Y'all goin' barbecue Memorial Day?"

"Probably, Earl got to have him some 'que on Memorial Day."

June 16th, Father's Day. He doesn't get the full kaduza, and more often winds up with a new tie or a pair of slippers than a feed bag.

And just when we had become accustomed to only minor league excursions into gluttonous behavior. July 4th. What is July 4th supposed to mean or do for African people in America?

I've been to barbecues (you have to go where your friends are) on July 4th, where the man of the house was flipping barbequed sauce, wearing a t-shirt that said, "We are not Independent or Free, yet."

I could repeat variations on that theme, followed by gigantic fireworks displays and a bunch of other patriotic madness.

The obesity, the tensions, the malfunctioning of the body that happens as a result of eating poison is evident as the nose on your face.

The Be'Helthi's have formed conclaves that are almost cult-elitist.

"Girl, I know wher you can find fresh bread!"

"I was talking to Johnny yesterday about bread."

Poor Be'Helthis, we have to be careful of our feelings, guard our sources before they are discovered and closed down for lack of the right license.

A Chinese friend of mine, a restauranteur and a Be'Helthi type told me that he was forced away from the good Cantonese style of cooking when he opened a restaurant on the westside.

"I tried to do it the way my parents had done it. Fresh vegetables, nothing overcooked, you know, real cuisine. People were bringing orders back saying that the food was not cooked well enough.

We had to change or else go out of business."

It should end there/here, but Fate demands that I mention sugar. Sugar...We even call each other "sugar," which is the only decent use of the term or the substance.

What's going to happen to us? The scenario is quite clear. We're going to eat ourselves to death without finding out what authentic food tastes like.

'Til taters get sweeter, Be'Helthi.

Changes

No place in the world is capable of changing as fast as Chicago. The whole city is a quick change artist.

It may have something to do with the weather. The Weather, as many people are fond of reminding us, will change at the drop of a hat.

It can go from cold to warm, from warm to cold (and often does, raining on one side of the street and not on the other side), it can sleet, snow, rain thunder and flash jagged bolts of lightening while the sun is shining.

The wind can blow you down, stand you back up and carry you to wherever you thought you wanted to go in minutes.

Neighbors are barometers of change in Chicago. You might have a Jewish neighborhood turn African-American (it has happened) or Mexican, or Czech neighborhood turn Mexican, or German neighborhood become Polish, or Lithuanian or Estonian or Croatian or Sorbian or Hindu Indian.

Strangely, the most stable neighborhoods seem to be mixed. Mixed with what? Well, who gives a shit! just mixed.

Tropical Intrigue

August is Chicago; the asphalt melts, heat waves shimmer on the horizon, people stay indoors with the fans fanning them or the air conditions on and drink beer and have lazy dog conversations about their neighbors, 'specially in the section called Blarney.

"Michael O'Reilly, you're as big a liar as I'd ever hope to find anywhere!"

"But its true, I tell ya! its true! Molly, come in here a moment will ya?"

"And what is it you'd be wantin', I'm tryin' to make soda bread, ya know, and its not the kind of thing that makes itself."

"I know darlin'," I know. But I need your witness."

"Well here I am, what is it?"

"I'm trying to tell the doubtin' Thomas here the truth about the people across the street."

"O Heavens! those ungodly folks! What about' em?"

"Remember when they were married to each other?"

"How could I ever forget?"

"Now just a minute, you're tellin' me that they once were married to each other?"

"They were married to each other, the man in that house was married to the woman in the house next door and vice versa."

"Saints preserve us!"

Coleen Ryan-Roberts stood on the enclosed porch of their new home, her arms folded defiantly across her firm Irish breasts. The bigoted bastards. You'd think they would simply accept us and go on about their business.

She out-stared the woman across the street and returned to the interior of her home. Time to prepare dinner, Clarence would be putting the car in the garage in a half hour.

She strolled slowly from the porch to the kitchen admiring the clean lines of the Danish sofa and table and comfortable chairs.

"Who the hell wants to eat feeling like they're in an electric chair."

The kitchen made her feel as though she were on a western ranch. Chile peppers were streaming down the walls beside the gas range, a giant chopping block gave her ample working space and all of the technological conveniences were strategically placed to make it a modern kitchen with an old fashioned look.

Fried chicken, steamed rice, a tossed salad. She walked over to the kitchen sink, stared out into the small garden they'd started at the beginning of the summer.

"I'm a southern boy, baby, we got to grow some greens 'n beans back there."

They had to give up on the garden after it was vandalized three times. The woman in the house next door smiled from her kitchen window and sprinkled a cheerful wave with her fingers.

Coleen waved and smiled back.

Thank God they're not all bigoted assholes. She turned from the window and pulled the package of chicken breasts from the refrigerator.

It wasn't easy being the first mixed couple in a predominantly Irish, working class neighborhood. They had seriously considered selling the house and going somewhere

153

else for the first six months.

"Coleen, are you sure you want go thru with this? Lets face it, with both of us working, you're going to be here alone a lot. Can you handle it?"

"Clarence I don't see colors, I see people for what they are and what we're looking at is a bunch of bigoted Irish bastards, my Dad, Lord rest his Soul, was a bigoted Irish bastard."

They were given the full treatment; garbage on the freshly cut lawn, crank calls and letters, mean looks and a few times, graffiti painted on the front door.

The hate treatment was never a full fledged community attack and gradually, with the aid of the local Catholic priest and the appeals made by right thinking neighbors at community meetings, the nasty treatment had simply degenerated to hate stare bouts with the woman across the street.

"Well, baby, looks like we're over the hump. We've had a whole month without one obscene phone call . . ."

"The tracer took care of that."

"No one has dumped garbage on the lawn."

"Seeing Father Maloney clean up the last time finished that off."

"And nobody has painted anything on the front door lately."

"Maybe they ran out of paint."

"I hope so."

They were left in social isolation. The lady in the house to the south of them smiled and waved from her kitchen window, but didn't extend her cordiality beyond that.

Coleen was given a harder time of it than Clarence. She could easily remember the slurs in the neighborhood supermarket; "Imagine, a nice lookin' red headed Irish girl married to a nigger."

154

"Is it really true, honey? That the darky got a bigger dong than us?!"

The social isolation bothered them because they both wanted friends in the neighborhood, the sense of belonging.

The isolation ended with the arrival of Frank and Melba Mackae. They purchased the house on the north side of them and they were also a mixed couple. He was white and she was black.

Clarence and Coleen peeked thru their drapes like excited children.

"Clarence, how do you know his wife is black?"

"Well, c'mon, you can't be that dark and not be black, not only that I saw'em kissin in the middle of their living room before they hung their drapes."

They impatiently waited a week before going next door with a batch of cookies and a welcoming speech.

They considered a number of nervous scenarios before making the approach.

"Clarence, what if they're not our kind of people?"

"Well, we won't kin til we find out, will we?"

"Coleen, can you imagine what it would be like if the whole block were full of mixed couples?"

"Clarence, what if she doesn't like me?"

"What're you talking about, if she doesn't like you?"

"Well, you know the kind of attitude some black women have about white women married to black men."

"I hardly think this black woman would have that kind of attitude, under the circumstances."

"Hi, my name is Clarence Roberts and this is my wife, Coleen...We'd like to be the first to welcome you guys to the neighborhood."

"C'mon in, we were wondering whether or not we should come over and introduce ourselves. I'm Frank Mackae and this is my wife Melba. C'mon in, we've got a really good bottle of wine to share.''

They had hit it off, as the saying goes. Clarence and Frank shared a conservative—boot strap philosophy that was not popular with African—Americans, in general, and white liberals, specifically.

"I'm with you there, Frank, we can't go around for the rest of our lives talking about how badly the slavemaster treated us.

I mean, gimme a break!''

Coleen and Melba didn't hit it off quite so well; but there was no really big problem between them. The basic area of disagreement was how they viewed their positions in their husband's lives.

"Coleen, why do you have to cater to Clarence like that? I mean, look, you're working and he's working. Why do you have to come home and cook and clean house and all of that while he does nothing but watch ball games on T.V.''

"Melba, I like catering to Clarence, its as simple as that.''

"Hmf! You won't see me doing all that domestic stuff by myself. We clean together or we clean apart.''

Despite the fact that they shared what they called "The mixed Couple Syndrome,'' the long fence they shared made them better neighbors.

Coleen poured a liberal amount of flour in a brown paper bag, sprinkled in salt, pepper and sage and dropped the chicken breasts into the bag, and shook them around the way Clarence had taught her.

"My mamma used to batter her chicken like this, its the best way in the world to get a nice even coating of batter on your chicken.''

Clarence felt, in this second summer of their relationship with the MacRae's, that they were on the way to a lasting friendship.

"I know, it isn't always easy to get along with Melba, but

lets face it, we don't have a perfect relationship either; and I love you."

They weren't particularly "avant garde" in any way. Frank was Scot; "My God! what am I doing but here in the middle of all these heathen Celtics?" And loved the whiskey after a hard day at the office.

He teased Coleen about being Irish; "if we Scots hadn't introduced you to Scotch, you'd still be drinking Irish whiskey."

And she teased him about being Scot.

"C'mon, tell me the truth, Melba, you're married to a Scotsman, where's the money buried?"

Melba and Clarence teased each other about being married to Coleen and Frank, gently, at first, and always privately.

"So, this is what it had to come to, huh? A freckled faced imitation of a sister."

"Whoooaaa! where are you comin from? I mean, how're you going to defend your marriage to the slavemaster? Or was he merely the overseer?"

Frank and Coleen never took it that far. Something else happened. They discovered their whiteness, during the course of a weekend tanning session.

Clarence and Melba had spent a few minutes in the sun over the course of the summer, and let it go at that.

Melba, you're already the color of my favorite eggplant, what the hell are you trying to prove?"

"And how about you, pal?"

Clarence had a golf morning and Melba went to get her nails done. Frank and Coleen were left in their sun tanning deck chairs, backs unsun-screened.

"Frank!"

"Yeah, what is it?"

"You think I could persuade you to come over here and splash some sun lotion on my back?"

157

Something about the way he gently rubbed the oil on her about—to—be—burned—back made Coleen look at Frank from another angle.

Clarence rubbed oil on her as though it were a chore, Frank understood. And when she rubbed oil on his back, he thanked her in a way that indicated she understood his skin in a way he had never had understood before.

"Coleen, you're a bonny lass, thanks"

A bonny lass? Clarence wouldn't be caught dead saying something like that.

Coleen measured rice into a pot, rinsed it. . . "No Uncle Bens for the kid, baby, I wanna have real ol' fashioned rice in my guts."

She discovered a kind of sensitivity in Frank that she was reluctant to admit, didn't exist in Clarence.

"Well, look, lets face it, Coleen, I'm sure a black guy must go thru sheer hell on the day to day level, just being black."

It started with an application of sun tan lotion to the back and escalated to stolen kisses in the kitchen during, social get togethers.

Coleen dropped a piece of chicken into a skillet of hot grease. The grease sputtered and popped.

They had become lovers a month ago, Coleen stared absently at the chicken frying. What the hell was it all about? Had they simply become lovers because they had black mates, something in common?

The irony of the whole idea made her smile. No, they hadn't become lovers because his wife was black and her husband was black, They had become lovers because they had fallen in love.

She removed lettuce, tomatoes, vinegar and oil from the refrigerator. She was in love with a man who wasn't her husband, a man who was married to someone else. But she didn't feel the shame she thought she would.

Frank was gentle, thoughtful, considerate and loved her.

"Coleen, I love you."

"I love you too, Frank, but there's nothing we can do about it."

"We can go away and start a new life together, I'm not rich but I have a little money coming to me from a trust fund."

She turned the pieces of chicken over in the skilled and began peeling leaves from the lettuce head into a salad bowl. For the tenth time that day she thought about Frank, about Clarence, compared the two men.

Clarence suffered thru the comparison; Frank was exquisitely sensitive to her sexual and emotional needs. Clarence had always been the kind of lover who placed himself on top physically and emotionally.

She had analyzed her reasons for marrying Clarence.

Number one, she concluded, she had married him to defy her racist parents and number two, he had been the first man to fully penetrate her. She had felt on obligation, as a practicing Catholic, to marry him.

But they definitely didn't have a case of "jungle fever," then or now. She heard a car pull into the back garage area, Clarence?

She peeked out of the rear window, Melba pulling in with packages. The woman must shop every day of the week. She turned back to the salad, began to toss it, turned the steamed rice off and began to fork pieces of chicken out of the skillet.

Damn! Life could be so complicated.

"Coleen, let me make something clear to you. I've been aware for quite awhile that Melba doesn't love me, maybe she never did. I think she saw me as a way to get a privileged break in this society, you know what I mean?"

"Lets face it, this is still a white man's country.

Coleen placed the salad in the refrigerator, covered the chicken platter with tin foil and wandered into the master bedroom and sprawled backwards on the bed.

Being with Frank was so beautiful, so easy. She cradled her head in her hands and stared at the ceiling.

Being with Clarence was always a challenge, a problem to be solved. There was never a time when she felt as much at ease with Clarence as she felt with Frank.

Maybe its because he's white. She spooned the thought around in her mind. Maybe it's because he's white. They had taken days off from work to be together and no one paid them any attention in restaurants when they held hands.

No one questioned their right to be together when Frank rented the hotel room. Life was much easier with Frank, no doubt about it. And I do love him.

"Coleen, this isn't something I planned either. How was I to know that I'd meet you. Lets face it, we're not wild eyed adolescents out for a cheap thrill."

She heard the garage door open and close, Clarence was home. She sat up on the side of the bed, a slight headache nudging into her temples.

She listened to her husband's movements, pictured his routine. He comes in, tosses his jacket across the back of the nearest chair, opens the refrigerator for a can of beer. She looked up to see him leaning against the door frame, one hand jammed into his pocked, the other one wrapped around a can of beer.

"What's for dinner?"

She smiled a welcome home smile that wasn't returned.

"Chicken, fried chicken and rice."

"Good, lemme get out of this suit 'n tie."

Coleen shuffled past Clarence entering the bedroom as she went to set plates on the dining room table, a dozen

160

conflicting thoughts on her brain. The faint scent of Opium lingered in her nostrils.

She ignored the signals that the perfume sent. Who in the hell am I to be jealous?

She blessed the meal as they sat opposite each other, exchanging general pleasantries, Clarence was drinking another beer and seemed more preoccupied than usual.

Had someone called him a nigger on the way home? It still happened occasionally, after almost two years.

"The chicken o.k."

"O, yeah, its good."

But she notice that he had only taken a few bites from his piece of chicken. He toyed with his salad and gulped his beer.

"Any more beer?"

"Some down at the bottom, I'll get it for you."

"Thats o.k., I can get it."

She detected a petulant tone, decided to ride it out. He returned to the table popping open a fresh can.

"We have some black walnut ice cream, if you want some dessert?"

Clarence sat down and leaned toward her with the beer can cradled in his hands, ignored her question.

"Coleen?"

God, the man looks tired. look at the circles under his eyes.

"Yes, Clarence."

He slugged more beer down, his eyes wandering from left to right.

"I want to talk with you."

"Yes, Clarence."

O my God, don't tell me he's been fired. Corporations were cutting a lot of "minority surplus" these days.

"What I mean is that I have something I want to tell you."

She leaned back in her chair. The least I can do is give him a shoulder to cry on, no matter what.

"What is it, Clarence?"

Once again his eyes darted from side to side like a trapped animal.

"Coleen, there's somebody else in my life," he blurted.

She leaned forward slowly, her lover jaw slack.

"Somebody...else...in ...your...life?"

"Now look, I felt the best thing to do is be honest about this. I'm not having a fling or anything like that. Its important that you understand that, this is the real thing...you understand what I mean?"

"I think so. And who is this somebody else, may I ask?"

She couldn't prevent the anger she felt from coloring her tone. Clarence drained his beer can and locked his eyes with hers.

"Melba MacRae."

He was startled by the manic flood of laughter she released. She was laughing so hard her sides hurt, tears came to her eyes. Clarence came around the table to comfort her.

"Coleen? look, I'm really 'n truly sorry about this. I never wanted to hurt you, you know that."

A half hour later he wasn't laughing after she calmed down enough to tell him why she had been laughing.

"Molly O'Reilly, if there's another woman this side of county Cork who makes soda bread half as good as you, give me her telephone number and I guarantee you my bachelor days will be over at the tender age of thirty three."

"There ya go again, Danny Ryan, wrappin' your spit around a bunch of compliments."

"Your soda bread is a great inspiration for that. But now tell me, Mike, how did these people wind up cross married, as it t'were?"

"Only God'n the saints in Heaven can answer that one..."

"The way it was told to me by Mary Flannagan, their next door neighbors over there, is that they had a meeting...can you imagine? And the black couple decided to move into the house next to Mary's and the white couple moved in next door."

"Most people who live in the neighborhood now don't know about these people."

"How long ago did this take place?"

"How long was it, Molly, 12—15 yrs. ago?"

"About that long, yes."

"And to further complicate things, take a close look sometimes, if you will, at their children. The black couple have a girl...how old is she about, Molly?"

"About twelve, I'd say."

"And the white couple have a boy about the same age.

The girl who belongs to the black couple looks Irish, and the boy looks black."

"You mean...?"

"That would be my guess."

"Saints preserve us!"

Coda—Chicago

(Maxwell Street/ Halsted Street) for some people it was the center of the known world, a Jewish souk, a place to go and buy cheap stuff cheap, or second hand stuff second hand.

Gypsies lived there, glittering, clairvoyant, deep. The most musical people in town gathered on the corner of Maxwell and Halsted to be fed quarters and dimes. Novels were written there, never to be read, hopes were realized.

Now we have tourists who come only to buy the Polish sausage sandwiches "with everything on 'em, the rumor is that the whole area is going to be "reborn." (Isaac B. Singer) I'd never heard of the man, to be honest with you, and if it hadn't been for this Jewish chick that I was dealing with I probably never would've heard about him.

"Kofi, you've got to read some of this man's stuff, it'll surprise you." So I read. And I was stunned into reading more. "The magician of Lublin" blew my mind.

"When he died in July of 1991 I felt kinda sad, you know what I mean? a little like a friend had passed on."

(Rap Love Song) "Passionate sweat made us both wet, I told you don't fret, a baby is not what you're gonna get... Passionate sweat made us both wet, remember I told you don't fret, a baby is not what you're gonna get ' cause I had the con—dom on.

You wanna have a orgasm!"

(Uncle Percy and Mr. Lloyd) "Right here where this ugly ass project stands is where 1150 Washborn used to be, or rather I should say, where the building we lived in used to be.

Basement, three floors and a left. We lived in the basement, pigeons lived in the loft. Seems like I could always find cracked pigeon's eggs that had rolled out of the loft and fell on the steps of the basement.

My uncle and aunt ran a gambling house on the weekends, from Thursday to Sunday morning, when she went to the little Baptist church up the street. No high blown rhetoric about the immorality of gambling, or any of that, people were trying to get by the best way they could.

The gambling scene fascinated the shit out of me, people arguing and grumbling and moving around a croupier table. I was especially fascinated by two particular gamblers, my Uncle Percy and a man named Mr. Lloyd.

Uncle Percy and Mr. Lloyd played one on one, a card game called "skin." I didn't know what "skin" was then and I still don't know what "skin" is.

These two men (uncle Percy, Gandhi thin and cool, Mr. Lloyd, pouchy eyed and warm) would sit across from each other after the croup shooters had gone and "skin" for a couple days.

Yes, two days at a crack. I still have the image of these two old men (they probably looked old from birth) sitting at the kitchen table, silently "skinning."

There were no whoops of joy for either of them when one lost and other won. It was a kind of zen thing.

The basic idea seemed to be on who could concentrate on something the longest. That was "skinning."

(47th street, The Peps) "There will never be, could never be another dance hall like the "Peps," I've been to all of 'em, Fillmore, the place in London, the Dand' Paris, up in Harlem.

Thing is I don't think the "Peps" was ever given the recognition it deserved. Harlem had the edge because it got the publicity but the Peps was equal to any of them.

It definitely had something to do with location, that much is certain. Forty-seventh Street just didn't have the same ring to it as one hundred thirty-fifth and Lennox, uptown. You know what I mean.?

Be that as it may, the place was magic. "Going up the steps" we called it. Rug lined staircase, a little tacky. We were searched by the security guard but it didn't prevent anything we wanted to bring in from being brought in.

The herb was smoked in the balcony and the cheap wine was drunk in the toilet.

Huge polished dance floor of springy wood, two monster speakers on either side of the stage, real beautifully dimmed lights. We danced in each others arms, pressed to each others bodies.

Many of us had our first sexual experience at the Peps. There were some girls there who could dance up against you so good it would make you cum.

No lie, there's documented proof of that. It was a tribal scene. On some Saturday nights when the D.J. was in a drum mood, he'd put one of those Chano Pozo type mambos on and send us back home. "He sent me out one night and I never returned."

(An "Old Timer" speaks)"It ain't about nothin' now. It ain't about nothin'. The sweet part has died, its all about dope and murder now.

Are you hip to a Black man named John Hendrik Clarke? I think he might be dead now but I went to a lecture he gave, years ago. And at this lecture he talked about what a civilization should be.

He made it plain 'n simple that industrialization did not mean civilization. Thats what most folks in the western world think civilization is.

He, said, "we have a civilization when people are civil to each other."

That statement has been ringing a bell in my head for years. I'm old enough to remember when we, Black people in Chicago, were relatively civil to each other.

Yes I know, there were always some uncouth types running around, but not like now. What happened?

Well, my personal opinion is that we surrendered our children to television. Let me explain what I mean.
I was at my son's house last week for dinner and the night after dinner, my grandchildren, Marvin, Sally and Tabula dashed downstairs to watch something on TV/VCR.

It was a tape of a rap group in concert. I sat on the sofa behind them and watched an hour and a half of uncivilized behavior.

There were no people with grey hair on the tape, no elders, just folks doing superfast dances and screaming profanity. I felt so sad I could of cried."

(Imani Blood Chicagoan)

So much positive stuff happens in this city every day that its unreal. Black people and white people are not strangling each other on sight, drug crazed gang members are not blazing away with Uzi's on every corner, the African-Americans here are not being left out of the political process and we are not going to hell this afternoon.

Sometimes I feel like screaming when I feel that I'm being saturated with all of the negative stuff. It comes from many directions; the media mostly, and from people who buy into the negative and spread it around.

No, of course, this is not paradise. We do have problems. That's intrinsic to city life.

But I refuse to allow the negative blinders to blot the positive picture art. We help each other here, people are ready, willing and able to do what they can to help the other person.

That's not an unusual thing, people do it ordinarily. We share. I think the greatest testimonial to the facts that most people in this city have their heads screwed on right is the fact that the city works.

If we were as messed up as some folks want to make us believe, we'd be up to our necks in shit. I rest my case.

We were blessed in 1991, to trip to Chicago, to retrace the motions and take a look at the sap rising. We watched the eggplant-colored people begin to glow, the butter yellows melt to brick-brown, the bleached ones acquire color.

Thunderstorms, saliva from the jaws of Heaven, sprinkled warm spit on us, nourished us. Distant flashes of jagged spear throwing, combined with cosmic atomic clashes scared the shit out of us.

Chicago's trees opened up on us, budding with hardened nipples that quickly bloomed into full flowering breasts.

The music drove us, came to us, surrounded us, penetrated us (Sarah Vaughn, Divinity, Channel 11/July 29th, 1991, 9:00PM), it was the blues, jazz, salsa, symphony, concerto, country, Croation, Subbulakshmi, Ramon Montoya, Nino Ricardo, Coltrane, the people next door that made us dance.

We danced, waiting for the traffic light to change. We fed on soul music, inner ear stuff. We danced for a while after the music had stopped.

Yes, of course, it was a nostalgic buy, irresistible for the price. Who wouldn't want to return to the place where they had first sampled snow-cones in the summer? Eaten hot slices of fire red watermelon, tasted Mississippi-made biscuits and made love to Odessa and Rose all summer.

Just to see Chicago Black style, to hang out with Bo-Manolete, doing a mental faena that few matadors have ever considered.

To go and check out the changes and be able to say, after the first winter hip leaf had been chipped from the tree, she's a beautiful lady and we saw her when she was putting her dress on, when she was dressed, when she started stripping and when she got naked. Ase.